The Soulless Man

A novella by

Innes Richens

ISBN: 978-1-7398607-0-7

This is a work of fiction. The characters, incidents, and dialogues are products of the author's imagination and not to be construed as real. The author's use of names of actual persons, living or dead, and actual places is incidental to the purposes of the plot and is not intended to change the entirely fictional character of the work.

Cover design from burconur via fiverr.com

Published by: deadhand

www.innesrichens.co.uk

Chapter 1
Winter

The heat of the summer's night clings to the walls of my room. From outside, through the small attic window, the distant tumble of the stream that runs down this narrow valley brings into this suffocating space the promise of cool air. The curtain, half drawn, does not lift, it hangs in the heat, heavy with it. There is a sheen across my chest, a thin dampness to the touch and my skin holds the sun of the previous day. I feel it rising from beneath the sheet, smothering my face. I push the sheet down to my waist, hoping for cooler air but the room has become bloated with this summer night. Everything is still, waiting, holding itself. My breathing is shallow and I slide my hand down to my belly, holding it there gently, feeling the slightest murmur of my heart, the rise and fall of my breath.

I open my eyes. The dark is still there. Gradually it softens and I see the outline of the window, the four small square panes and beyond a deeper night. The land stays silent as the summer spreads like honey. I focus on the sound of the stream, bringing the lightness of it into my head, willing it to lend the coolness of its water to my skin.

Eventually, I feel the skin beneath my hand ease away from the heat. Then – oh joy – the thin curtain seems to shift. I watch it, wondering if it was a trick of the light. It moves again, the light tendrils of a breeze across my chest, the faintest running of air. A summer breeze has found our small valley and begins to run between the houses, gently teasing at the windows.

The room's stale smell of fabric, old carpet, dust and adolescence is gently teased apart and I can smell the land beyond, the meadows and fields, the trees of the thin copse that threads its way up the valley lane. The curtains lift again, a definite movement now, I hear the fabric brush against the frame. I take the first deep breath and close my eyes, floating into half sleep, my body both woken and assured by the shifting of the heat. The stream is a constant gentle rhythm, it expands in my head until it fills my senses and follows me into sleep.

Cold. The unfamiliar sting of it, the confusing grip of it on my shoulders, across my lips. I am awake before I open my eyes, instinctively clutching to draw the sheet up over my bare skin. I open my eyes.

The room is brighter and at first I struggle to understand what it is that is making it so. It is not the light of dawn, it is harder than that, fixed, determined. Everywhere in the room, there is a cold blue light carefully coating my desk, the bookcase, the chest of drawers. My eyes focus out of their sleep. There is ice everywhere, a thin hard coating of it covers the room. Patches of it mark the carpet and when I pull at the sheet I disturb a thin coating that has settled over me. It's shards and fragments are shattered around me, between the shape of my legs. My breath frosts in the air. I sit up, instinctively reaching for the bedside light but I pause and don't switch it on. Everything is still and a fear of flooding it all with artificial light stops me. The absence of the stream's constant tumbling deepens the silence. Nothing moves. My skin has tightened across my chest, my breathing is shallow. I move, the cold pushing me out of bed. I grab for the clothes that are on the battered chair in front of the bookcase. They are cool, damp, a slight brittleness as I first touch them however they soon warm me and I begin to think more clearly.

I wonder if the whole house has been covered in this thin, new ice and I slowly open the bedroom door. The narrow stairs that lead down to the main landing stand cold and silent, the handrail glistening with patches of frost, mould-like in their creeping shapes across the wood. I can feel the carpet crunch gently beneath each step as I carefully descend, aware that it is still night, that my parents and brother are in nearby rooms, not wanting them to wake to this, feeling that – somehow – I would be blamed, that it would then be the family's drama, removing it from me, my own private experience. I suddenly remember the dog. She sleeps in the small hall, near the back door. Part of me wants to get her, her presence confirming this is happening, lending me some sense of security.

The main hall is glittering, the ice catching what must be moonlight, steady and pale, coming through the arch of the window above the front door. The house at night is another place, empty of the lives that fill it with movement and noise. The place waits, colour is muted shadows. The ice covers everything - even the pictures of racing horses, their bodies broad, rectangular, each leg awkwardly, improbably arranged, the frosted glass distorting the uneven shapes.

I am aware I do not know why I have come downstairs, where I am going. The door to the lounge, the front door, the stairs behind me, these all present me with a decision I have not anticipated. The night remains silent, giving no explanation, and I stand in the small hall on a rug glistening with a heavy frost, wondering what to do next. Until now, I have not considered the improbability of what I am seeing, but the cold tease of the air around my neck, in my nose, this is real and constant. I cannot dismiss it as waking confusion.

I put my hand gently on the front door's heavy handle and feel the sticky freeze of ice. Standing close to its solid wood panels I can sense the wide night beyond, a deeper, older cold stretched out across the land and I feel pulled towards it.

Ignoring the pull of the flesh on my fingers, I turn the key and slowly ease the heavy door open, wary of the dog, the others sleeping above me, and step out into a night bright with moon and snow.

The path that runs from the house through the brief, plain garden before the less organised ramble of the lane is covered and even with snow, it's brittle surface blue with ice. There is silence hanging from the trees along the lane, clinging to the house behind me, it is a silence full of space, the still air full of expectation, like a held breath. The cold is deeper, firmer than the sharpness in the house. I pull the zip of my hoodie closer to my chin and the hood up over my head. My feet begin to feel the coldness of the earth through the soles of my trainers and I briefly wish I had put on socks.

It is not the even path I choose, but the smaller, narrower one that leads to the side gate, the one that opens on the drive, it's slope muted by snow. The metal of the gate grabs the skin of my hands as I open it, waiting for the grating squeak of its slanting hinges. Nothing happens and the night seems to watch me as I step through the deeper snow of the lane. Only in my movement there is noise, my footsteps a muffled push, brief and dull, quickly stifled in the heavy stillness of the valley.

I have no idea where I am heading, just an urge to keep moving, to take it all in, this frozen landscape, this cold little valley, its trees climbing the steep slope, brittle with ice catching at the frozen air. Nothing moves, the moon is still and nearly full above the valleys edge. There is a rough stile set into the hedge, it's dark crumbling step glistening in the cold. I delicately cross it, into the darker path between the trees, that makes a ragged way up the hillside, winding into the silence. My breath grows heavier with the climb, clouds in the air in front of me, catching the moon's light as it falls between the branches.

At the top of the valley, a plain little field, covered in an even, bright layer of snow and I hesitate at the tree line, unwilling to step into the wide, unprotected space. The top of the snow brittles with broken light where the gentle rolling of the land pushes from hedgerow to distant hilltop.

From the corner of my eye, over to the right, where the far edge of the field follows the final curve of the wood, a movement, made more obvious, more stark to me by the stillness that has settled heavily across everything. There is a figure moving along the tree-line, tall, steadily plodding as it breaks the crust of snow with each careful step. I cannot make it out against the dark edge of trees behind it but I can hear the soft footsteps in the snow, coming to me across this still field. I stay very still. Before too long it will reach the end of the trees, where the hill breaches and tumbles way across other fields, towards the next valley. There it will be silhouetted against the moonlit sky and I will see its shape more clearly.

I feel an ache in my throat, my chest and realise I have not let go the breath I took on first noticing this strange figure. Slowly I breathe out, trying to make no noise, trying to make no cloud of breath in the cold air. The figure has reached the skyline and I see more of its shape. It is oddly angular, ungainly in the way it moves its arms, its legs seem to fold and buckle in an awkward manner as it haltingly continues along the hilltop, where the path that hides beneath my own feet will take me.

As it reaches the bare hilltop, it stops and I can see it is unnaturally tall, even though it appears to bend over, its long arms thin, almost sweeping the ground. I cannot see its head, just a dim shape above the shoulders. It stops and I am filled with a sense that it is aware of me, that it sees me, here, faltering at the hedge, that it has known I was here all along. I half expect it to gesture me towards the hilltop, to beckon with long, awkward arms. I stay where I am, although the urge to run away is strong, to run from this place, to turn and slide down into the familiarity of my valley. I cannot move, though, even though the freezing wood of the stile has numbed my fingers to the first glimmering of pain.

The figure unfolds its arms, lifting them slowly above its head. They seem to be full of joints and bends, their jutting shape reaching to wrap around the unmoving silence of the moon above us both. My heart begins to pulse in my throat and I lose all sense of the cold. The moment hangs in the silent field, amongst the branches and then the air is suddenly full of noise, a high and desolate scream pushing like a wave from the figure on the hilltop. It vibrates in my bones and fills my mouth and eyes with the shock of it and I cannot breathe. The sharpness of the air catches it and pushes it across the field and into the sky, filling everything with its desperation until I feel it pushing at me, my legs giving way to it. I feel my hand slide from the fence, the coldness of the ground as my knees sink into the snow. I cover my ears and still feel it running through my body like a wave that has caught me, pushing me out into the cold dark.

I wake to the morning light. And heat. The sheet on my bed is wrapped around my legs, my boxers have curled and twisted around my hips. I am hard with the urge to pee and my hair is wet against my forehead. Through the open window sound and noise has returned to the world – the running of the valley stream as familiar as my breath, a neighbour's kid chattering away as a car is loaded. I lay still, disorientated, sensing my heartbeat, slow, strong, steadying itself. The summer that settles around me, around this house is bewildering after all that ice and snow, the cold, steely moonlight seems impossible now against the evidence of my working senses.

Eventually the muffled sounds of movement in the kitchen, the clatter of cupboards and drawers motivates me to get out of bed. They are so familiar they push me into the usual morning routine while my mind still turns over the intensity of… what? a dream? Such vivid, short experience, the sharpness of the cold in each breath, the rigid smell of frozen earth, the darkness of the shadows picked out in slanting moonlight on snow. The force of it felt too large, too overwhelming to me for it to be just a dream, and yet here I am, putting on shorts, a T-shirt in the early heat of a summer's morning. I reach for my trainers, sliding my bare feet into them and feel the shock of cold, the sucking dampness and quickly my skin goose-pimples and, sharply, that scream lifts from somewhere in my subconscious to widen my eyes briefly before another shout, closer, more familiar, comes from the bottom of the stairs. "Boys! Breakfast! Come on!"

It is my mother. I hear the hall door rattle shut as she heads back to the kitchen. I leave the wet trainers on the floor, going barefoot, not wanting their dampness on me. I head to the bathroom for a pee. My hair is tousled, clinging around my ears and I ruffle it through. I can smell my body, still wrapped in the warmth of my bed. As I pass my brother's door I knock.

"Come on Ollie, stop what you're doing, put it away and come downstairs for breakfast "

I know that will annoy him. He is a year younger than me. He hates to be reminded that I know, that I have gone ahead of him, that nothing he does is new or private to him. It doesn't matter if it's true or not, it matters that I know.

"Dan, are you going to cut the lawn today? You promised your father you would" my mother says. The emphasis on my name seems unnecessary. My father sits at the kitchen table, reading a paper. It is his way of keeping the newer aspects of the world in its place, insisting on a real paper, foregoing a tablet as if world described in print is somehow more true. However, the only paper he can get delivered now is the local one, full of stories about school productions, a farmer selling land, an incident between a car and a cyclist, lists of prizewinners at recent shows. He looks up at me and gives a brief "morning". He says nothing about the lawn.

Mum is bustling, pots and plates are moved, drawers opened, teapots swirled. The table is already laid with cereal, juice, jams and marmalade. A mug of tea is placed in front of me as I sit.

"Where is your brother? Did you call him?" she says, doing something in the sink "Do I need to go and fetch him?" At this point, Ollie appears, still in his boxers, a rumpled T-shirt, rubbing his eyes with sleep.

Breakfast proceeds like hundreds of breakfast before it, it's normality more stark than usual, more comforting in a strange way. Over toast I negotiate my day, it's to be lawn first, then, later a swim, just before the pool closes when I know it will be quieter, the kids gone home for their tea.

Chapter 2
Swim

The water in the pool is just cool enough to make my skin tighten. Its surface is beginning to settle from a day full of excited kids and groups of pensioners standing in the shallows. There are a few others in the lanes that mark off one side, steadily doing their lengths or loitering at the end of a lane, taking a few breaths. I push off from the ladder, out into the relative calm of the open water. The water feels good across my shoulders, my legs, after the heat of the day, after sweating away over the old lawnmower, struggling it around the uneven slopes and ragged corners of the lawns. I dive under feeling the water close over the top of my head, the hollow echoes and noise of the pool suddenly muted and all I hear is the rushing of my own blood. The tiles of the floor slope away to dimmer waters and I follow the darker line marking the lane, moving slowly, enjoying the feel of my body being gently stretched and flexed. Eventually I float to the surface and the noise of large, open space above me cuts back in and fills my head. I turn over onto my back and look up at the ironwork that crosses the roof. It is an old building, built when it mattered that even such functional elements as the roof girders had some flourish. Despite my goggles and poor eyesight, I can see the orderly curls and decorative edges of it all and beyond, behind the dirty glass panels, the early light of evening.

I should be starting my routine, the steady beat of laps but something holds me here in this moment of floating, letting the water lift me, easing muscle and bone, washing away the day. There must be a cloud crossing over because the light dims, barely perceptible but just enough to push my mind back to the night before. A quick chill that speaks of snow and moon runs across my chest. It makes me instinctively turn and swim towards the deep end, using the movement to break the thought, to chase away a memory of a cold hilltop, a gaunt figure, a howl.

The water in the deep end feels cooler and I sense the weight of it below me. There is no one down here and the clap and chatter of the surface has settled. The noise of the place echoes all around me and I dive into the dimmer depths, opening my eyes to search at the bottom of the pool. Faded by the darkening blue of the water, the light pushing through but giving way, something moves at the corner of my vision. I turn to look, fighting the urge to dart back to the air. There, near the deepest part, where a filter cover marks the bottom, there is a patch of dancing light like sun on the ruffled surface of a lake, a ripple of laughter in a darkened room. There must be sunlight somewhere above, breaking through the industrial glass, striking down to this patch of the pool. I move towards it, aware my breath will hold just for a short while before the deep urge to breathe overwhelms me.

The patch of light does not seem to get its source from anywhere above, there is no tell-tale beam of sun striking down to the cooler waters. It seems self-sustaining, like seeing a summer's day through the back door of a quiet house. I am nearly above it now and I notice, as I hover there, I cast no shadow. The light seems to grow, creeping across the tiles, spreading out, gently brightening. I can make out its edges now, they seem definite, real. I reach out towards it and find I can grasp it, feeling a firm threshold. Instinctively I pull myself through, my lungs now beginning to signal their urgency and I flow through easily into colder water. There is soft light everywhere and, impossibly, above me green and blue, a surface. I kick towards it, breaking into air, letting go of my breath with a soft explosive sigh before breathing in a scent of earth and trees, the unmistakable freshness of being outside.

There is a tree cascading its long thin branches into the water, its leaves a delicate, tenuous green. The light is that of a late summer's afternoon as the sky turns towards a long evening. Above me, more branches, a canopy of green alive with small motion and the sky above shimmering through. I tread water and breathe, my heart has not yet steadied from the pounding of a breath held too long. The water clings lightly to my skin, runs softly from my face, and the smell of growth, of life lifts from it, the sharp chlorine of the swimming pool giving way.

I do not try to make sense of it, each time I approach any attempt, my throat tightens, I feel my stomach clench. Instead I swim to the near bank, a shallow strip of rock and coarse sand that fades into the grass of the woodland.

I sit on the low edge of earth, letting the water run from my legs, rivulets across my broad feet like veins. The pool is narrow, it gently curves around the trees either side of me, passing out of sight. Although there is an occasional breeze, I do not feel cold and there is enough sun rippling through the trees to warm me, I feel the light touch of it across my shoulders, my legs. My skin soon dries though my shorts still cling to me. I stand and look behind me into the woods. I see there is a suggestion of a path, its edges faded by new growth, tantalising as it curves out of my sight. I begin to follow it, picking my way with the awkwardness of bare feet. Trees quietly surround me.

The sound of running water reaches me, twisting in between the trees, the splashing run of a stream. Ahead the light grows stronger, more confident. There is a clearing and I pause at its edge. It is a small area, overgrown with bracken and the twists of plants. In the centre the earth rises to enfold itself gently around the structure of stone, roughly built but old, solid. It looks like a house that has been half built, left unfinished, three walls reaching above me. The fourth has tumbled away its stones, scattering them into the undergrowth. Empty windows, the lintels softly arched sit uniformly in each wall. There is no roof and rising from the centre of the building, a large willow tree, its branches draping and caressing the stones. I move quietly around the edge of the clearing to see what might be inside. The sound of running water fills the air with a lightness, full of cool promise on a hot day.

The willow sits in the centre of the structure, its branches parting over a small pool at its base, a small stream eases from it, falling through the clearing towards me. The sun presses unhindered on my shoulders, its heat pushing at my skull, teasing through my hair. I move instinctively into the shade of the tree, drawn to the calmness of the pool, stepping into the shallower end where it narrows to the beginning of the stream. The water is warm, my skin responds with a gentle flush, spreading up my thighs and I wade towards the deeper water, towards the gentle, broad twist of the willow's trunk. The bottom of the pool feels like a fine sand over firmer rock. There is a heat rising from the earth below and I notice, all around me, the bubbling and bursting of springs rippling the surface of the pool. My foot finds one, an insistent pulse of warm water up through the rock and I pause, letting the heat of it roll up my leg, running inside my shorts, spreading across me and I feel myself respond to its insistent gentle pressure.

Here where the pool is deepest, under the spreading dome of the willow, I half float in the green light, looking up through the branches, seeing the distant whiteness of the sky, the branches and long delicate leaves in constant motion . The embrace of the spring coils around me, teasing at every inch of me now and I hold still, letting it explore me, letting my body respond. There is a hard urgency in my belly now, my breath is shallow, quicker, my skin has tightened across my chest. The teasing of the waters, the restless flickering of the tree above me, it becomes a rhythm deep inside me until I hear myself moan softly, instinctively. I resist the urge to close my eyes, to lay back into the waters, to open my legs wide. I resist but I do not want to, I want to let it happen. The moment comes and I gasp as I release my breath, feeling the warmth of it hot and sudden. My breathing becomes deeper, slower and the light around me settles, clarifies itself into branches, the green light on leaves, the waters of the spring. I bring my hands to my face splashing water on it washing away the sweat and I stand slowly, looking around guiltily expecting to be observed. There is nothing but the light, the tree, the constant motion of the spring and stream.

A small movement, just on the edge of my hearing, quick and brittle against the wide open space of the forest. I look up, my eyes shrink briefly from the light as it glitters and dances between the leaves. Somewhere up in the branches, a quick sharp flutter of movement, a bird perhaps as it picks its way between the thinner branches higher in the tree. It is the first sense of other life I have seen since my arrival and my focus sharpens quickly around it. There, above and to the left of me, a small shape, dark against the brightness, bustling between the branches. It has the dry, quick movement of feathers, a darting presence amongst the pale leaves. The light is too strong behind it for me to make out anything other than its small dark form, a knot of shadow. There is a suggestion of wings, their feathered ends flicking sharply but there seems to be too many of them, darting out awkwardly and frequently from its body at many angles. It seems to be clambering though the flowing maze of the willow, towards me, making its insistent way to me. As it nears, a soft whispering begins to rise above the deeper sound of the spring, a sibilant murmuring. I can't make out the words, it is a constant repetition, the same rhythms making themselves over and over, weaving toward me.

The shape is climbing towards me, on the lower, firmer branches now its progress less clumsy, more sure. The whispering has become insistent, the structure of it clearer. It is a sentence, repeated gently, the words are unfamiliar to me, a language of the throat and tongue. The creature has stopped and sits on a branch just above me. I still cannot make out its form in any detail, its silhouette giving away a jangled, irregular gathering of feather and bone. If it is watching me there is nothing in its shape to suggest eyes or a face, but the sense that it is here because I am here flickers through it. The constant whispering may be coming from this creature, but the running sound is laced between the willow leaves and so seems to fall all around me.

Then the whisper stops and it is as if the world takes a gentle breath inwards, holding briefly - the spring, the forest, all settle into a brief silence before a clear, light voice speaks the phrase into the stillness, no longer whispering, emphatic, each word formed lightly.

With a sharp crackling of feathers the creature tumbles from its branch, diving into the pool beside me, the crash of it shocking against the settled noises of the glade. Instinctively, I know I do not want to be in this pool with that creature and I quickly wade, half-swim to the shallower shore, my legs tensing with the anticipation of a sharp grasping of a hard, beak, talon or the dry scratch of feathers. I scramble from the pool, the water streaming from my shorts, down my legs and I turn to watch its waters. Its surface settles from my splashing exit, back to the gentle roll of the springs. Nothing else moves there. The green light filtering through the willow is gentle, settled.

I realise I am holding my breath, I let it go and take another, slower and deeper. There is nothing now. I want to leave, the subtle peace of the place now holding an uneasy edge, there is a feeling of being watched, pursued even, clinging to my drying skin. The path that brought me here fades away into the trees and I pick my way along it. The trees, the light, the soft still air are around me but it feels scented with something, and earthy, insistent yearning pull at me. I realise I have crossed my arms protectively around my chest, hunching forward. My shorts are still damp, clinging to me and this makes me feel more naked than I am.

The first curving pool is still there, calm, the mayflies scattering as I wade in. I have no real idea whether this is how I return, I simply retrace my steps until the cool waters fold around my shoulders. With a deep breath I sink my head into the dark and the green. I don't know what else to do, I float just under the surface and brace myself to open my eyes, hoping something will show me the way.

There is a sudden clasping grab at my arm, the shock of such a definite sensation running across my shoulder, up my neck. My head swims with it and then, other hands under my arms, rough, urgent and I feel lifted, the water falling away from my body. The noise that breaks into my head as I clear the water is a jagged disarray of echoes and shouts.

"Get him over here. No, on his side" a confident voice, a woman. There are hands around my ankles now and I feel my body laid on a cold hard surface.

"Hello? Can you hear me?" the voice again and cool fingers pressing the side of my throat "Nod or open your eyes if you can hear me?"

I do open my eyes and the light is cold, steady and with it comes the harsh, clean smells of a swimming pool. I suddenly take a breath.

"He's breathing" another voice, nearby, male.

"What's your name?" the woman again, her voice softened with relief "Can you hear me?"

I nod and mumble my name. The world is reasserting itself and with it the realisation that I am the centre of a drama, there are people standing around me, I can see their feet. Somewhere nearby there is a smaller, thin voice on a radio, asking for an update. The man's voice answers "Its OK, no need, you can stand that down, he's looking OK."

"Hello Dan, just stay still for a moment, everything's fine" the woman, her face now in my field of view, her hair tied back, smiling though her eyes still have a shadow of concern, "You gave us a bit of a fright"

A blanket is put across my shoulders. My head is clearing and with it comes a building sense of embarrassment. I don't know what has happened but I know I am suddenly at the centre.

"I'm OK, I'm OK, its OK" I say and I begin to sit up, holding out my hand to signal to the woman that everything is ok as she moves instinctively to stop me.

"He's looking better, his colour's back" she says to someone, or anyone, standing nearby, "Think we're ok now. Show over."

They won't let me leave by myself and I have to sit in the reception, on show, while they call my mother to fetch me. I feel fine now, but the crushing sense of embarrassment is like a force pushing me to go, now, away from this place, out into the wider world where no-one knows this has happened.

Of course I tell no-one. The last few days have been full enough of gentle teasing about my episode in the pool. Its typical of me, apparently, and I'm an idiot - according to my family. I am sure there is a concern somewhere behind it all, that the pointed humour is perhaps a fumbling way of checking how I am, of checking that normal life has resumed.

Chapter 3
Sash

I escape, taking the bike out, heading out of the narrow little valley towards the scrambling edges of the nearby market town. I am going to see Sash, we messaged each other last night and decided to meet up. At college she's known as Encore! or SashEncore!, after some old trance tune, but I just call her Sash. She's in my history class, that's how we met. We sat next to each other on that first day and I remember her turning to me to say hello as she opened her laptop.

She has a sort of ordinariness about her that I like, it is genuine, there's no pretence to be anything which, in the heaving world of high school relationships and politics, is unusual, perhaps unique. If I'm honest with myself, I feel safe around her, as if I can relax and forget to pay attention to all the hidden rules about how you are supposed to behave.

Sash is a lesbian. I don't remember this ever being announced, any grand reveal, no coming out video or speech, she's just always been a lesbian, so much so that everyone just knows it, it is as part of her as her short hair or the subtle braces on her teeth that you can see - if you look - when she smiles. Which happens often. The laugh that comes from her is large, loud, surprisingly so for her slight figure.

The day is a calm one, a blue sky, the clouds few and high. It is still early and the smell coming from the passing hedgerows still has night lingering amongst the warming of the green and the grasses. There is still dew clinging in some corners and, where the lane dips, the air cools slightly.

Sash lives in a bungalow on the edge of town. Her mother works in the local hospital. I've never met her dad, who left when she was still a baby. Sash mentions him occasionally, there doesn't appear to be any bitterness in her about his absence, perhaps that is still to come.

I prop the bike against the gate post at the end of her drive. The small garage door is open and Sash is wheeling her bike out of its dimness.

"Dan Dan such a Man!" she says, so accustomed to saying it that it falls lightly around us.

"SashEncore!" I respond, it's allowed.

"All right?" she looks down to adjust a pedal, "Where we off to? Some wild adventure? Some mystery need solving?"

She smiles at me, her choice of words making me falter inside but she obviously can't know.

We decide to head into town first to get supplies and then out into the sprawling countryside to the south, where the valleys and, importantly, the steep lung busting hills have smoothed. The day is huge, wide, open skies that wrap around the edge of our world as we cycle through the rolling lanes and jumble of fields. There is the first real warmth of summer running through everything and I can soon feel my shirt clinging to my shoulders, the small of my back. We talk as we ride, nothing momentous, nothing too thoughtful. It is easy and free of anything except those moments of idle friendship. Sash laughs, short huffs and bursts between deeper breaths. The lanes are relatively flat as the land settles towards the river, towards the south.

We are not aiming for anywhere in particular, simply riding and being somewhere that is not our usual places. Without consciously acknowledging it we take every small side lane we come across, letting the maze of them draw us in. As we pass through a small wood there is a rough lay-by formed through cars and tractors pulling off the tarmac, the grass has worn away in a shallow arc, the undergrowth and trees held back around an untidy smear of rubble and dirt. Stopping the bikes means the noises of travel, of the push of tires and pedals and the constant rush of air, it all disappears and the sudden quiet makes us stand silent for a few moments.

From somewhere in the wood the sound of a small stream comes tantalisingly through the trees and, for a moment, I get a pulse in my stomach that threads itself up my spine, the memory of a pool and a willow tree threatening to push itself upon the day.

"Coffee time I think" Sash says and she is already unhooking her rucksack from her shoulder and pushing her bike into the soft green of the copse. We leave the bikes propped against a tree, tangled together and sit next to the stream. Sash has kicked off her shoes and her feet are wavering fish in the stream. I want to take off my shirt, its dampness cooling now, but I am awkwardly aware of exposing skin even around Sash so I let the sweat slowly roll into the pit of my back and hope the cooler air of the wood will dry me out quickly.

We drink coffee from Sash's thermos. The cafe in town transformed itself a year ago from a place of formica tables, spilled sugar and the smell of frying to one of wooden floors, the smell of baking and fresh coffee, the constant hiss of an expresso machine. They filled our flask with hot, dark coffee and wrapped large slabs of rough apple cake in paper for us and we sit and eat these, our mouths so full we do not talk.

To say that I love Sash would be too much, too large for what I feel. We fell easily into our friendship, never really talking about it, just letting it happen. Our friendship has always felt like this, unadorned by any complications of attraction as if somewhere near our start we agreed to set that all aside. Sash's love of girls has always just been there and so there was never any doubt that our relationship was anything more than friendship. It removed the unknown edges that others might have knocked themselves against.

"Sash" I say looking at her feet. She makes some gentle sound, her yes closed in the filtering light. "Have you ever wondered if there's …" I falter, suddenly feeling self conscious, "Um, if there's something else behind all this?"

Sash doesn't make a sound, she doesn't move at all, just stays there with her head slightly to one side. I relax. I know by her silence she is thinking about it. The absence of some immediate, gently sarcastic response means she will answer, that she's interested.

Eventually she opens her eyes to look at the ruffling waters of the stream flowing through her toes and says "Yes, I think so" It is a gentle yes and my heart feels confirmed. "I hope there is anyway. It would be pretty grim if there weren't."

She looks at me, smiling, pausing, an invitation to go on.

"Mmm, yes" I say and, after a pause, "Have you ever had any proof of it? I mean actual experience of it?"

"What? Like something spooky? A ghost or some weirdness?"

I nod and shrug at the same time, unsure now where I intended to take this conversation. The stream, the trees, the gentle light are all a constant around us both, oblivious to us.

Sash looks across the stream and says, "Well, no, not really. My mum goes to church. She's sort of religious. But I think she just likes the people, the social side of it all. She doesn't really talk about the god stuff"

She pauses, draws one foot out of the water and inspects her small toe, brushing the rivulet of water from the soft skin. "I've not really been that much into the god and churches thing. But, yes, I do want there to be something else, you know, something. Something behind all this. Why? Have you seen stuff?"

Its the natural question and I should know its coming but I am unprepared for it, I haven't thought about how to tell it. However the moment seems ready for it.

"Maybe. I'm not sure. There's been some weirdness" I laugh gently and part of me wants this conversation to tumble off into a jokey, short lived moment that passes "I don't really know what to make of it really."

Sash looks at me now, no hint of anything on her face, just a look of conversation, of interest. So I tell her, clumsily, about what happened at the pool, about the threshold of light and the strange creature of feathers. I leave out a lot of detail, feeling uncomfortable about the intimacy it suggests. "All a bit weird. And embarrassing"

Sash has returned to looking at her feet in the water "You poor thing" she says, "Do you think you just passed out underwater?"

I nod, perhaps this is it, perhaps it is nothing more than that and Sash is right. I don't feel dismissed though I do feel reluctant to disagree. Eventually the other story comes out, the dark hill under a cold moon, the gaunt shape and the howl, its limbs reaching into the sky. As I tell it, I can hear myself, as if from a distance, trying to pick the words that do not give away too much of me, of the fear I felt, still feel, of the deep chill it has left inside me. Sash listens, watching the waters across her feet.

When I have finished, we sit for a while listening to the delicate webs of bird song around us.

“Do you think it’s a, I don’t know, a message? Maybe?” she says and with her question I feel the first gentle thrill of adventure, of a mystery shared and laid out before us like an uncovered map.

“Yeah, but what message?” I say. Sash hums briefly in response and nods, then rests her chin on her knee.

“Sure, exactly” she says and she looks at me “I guess that’s what we need to find out then?”

We don’t speak of it any further, the day is too clear and calls to us and we get back on our bikes and head further into the land There is no destination other than the here and now, the broken small lanes that have long been forgotten by most traffic. The aim is not to get there but to be out, away from our usual worlds. We stop at lunch time in a small meadow that is gradually filling with wild flowers, wheeling the bikes inside the sagging gate, we settle in the centre, letting the long grass gently embrace us as we eat.

As we lay there Sash breaks the easy silence “Next time it happens, call me right?”

“Next time?” I am alarmed, I had not contemplated it happening again.

“Yeah, next time” she says, shrugging her shoulders “There’s bound to be one, if its a message, because you haven’t understood it yet”

Sash’s matter-of-fact tone does little to assure me and my mind begins to turn and tumble the proposal of it over and over, worrying at it like a bead.

"Just call me" she says "Afterwards. We can try and decipher it"

"OK" and there must be something in my voice because Sash turns her head to me and says "It'll be ok. If its a message, they want you to hear it."

I give a sort of nervous half laugh and sit up.

"They?" I say and she just smiles at me "Sure. OK. I'll call you. If it happens". I sigh.

The day is gently turning towards its afternoon. I feel oddly relaxed, despite the turning thoughts of it all. Sash's presence feels good.

The sun is beginning to tilt towards the high tree-line of the surrounding hills by the time we arrive back at Sash's house. There is a car in the driveway now, her mum is home from her shift and there is a vague, enticing smell of spices drifting from the house. The clatter of cooking softly curves towards us from the windows.

"Do you want to come in?" Sash says as she leans her bike into the darkness of the garage "Mum will have cooked enough to feed the whole town."

I smile and say no, my own mother will be expecting me.

"OK. Good adventure Danny Boy. We should do it again" she says. We hug briefly and I begin to push my bike towards the lane.

"Don't forget to call me when the spooks come back!" she calls after me. Her smile is broad and I laugh and wave her down with one flap of my hand then, with a swing of my leg, I am on my bike, off into the creeping evening.

Chapter 4
Mr Hardy

Mr Hardy has positioned his desk in front of the large, wide window that overlooks the small car park in front of the college. His room is long and narrow and the desk too large, the dark expanse of it reaching so close to each wall that Mr Hardy will have to turn sidewise to get past.

The day behind the window is bright, an even white sky washes across view. There are trees, they run along the front of the college's boundary but from where I sit I can't see them, only the white of the sky and the even squares of the window. And Mr Hardy.

He looks small against the dark width of the desk. He has chosen a high backed chair, so all I see of him is the outline of broad, thick shoulders and his head against the window's light. I am sitting in a chair designed purely for function and even though I am tall it feels as if my feet do not touch the ground, that they are swinging nervously like a child's. I place my hands on my thighs to check - my feet are not swinging, they are crossed and tucked under the chair.

"So, Dan, we need to discuss your timetable." he says. He is looking at me and I know he will be adopting what he believes is a stern, professional yet understanding face but I can only see the outline of his red hair, the regularity of his side parting. I nod.

"You've put down that you want to do … let's see" he picks up some papers, pretending to study them as if he does not know, as if this is a casual conversation, soon sorted. "Yes, you want to do Biology and Chemistry … good .. And English." There is a slight accent when he says English, as if the word is unfamiliar in his mouth. He looks up at me, I am expected to confirm.

"Yes. I like English" I say. It sounds weak when I hear it though it is the truth.

"I see" he says and puts the papers down "Well, we want to support our students, enable them of course …"

He says words. I listen. They are about capability, raising ambitions, excellence. He talks about advising and choices in the here and now that affect our lives in the long term. He keeps saying 'we' whenever he refers to the college, giving me the impression that the whole staff have somehow discussed me and my choices and I briefly wonder what Lou, who works the till in the canteen, has said about me. Then he talks about balance, about the college's responsibilities versus the individual. I am listening but the weight in my chest tells me the answer is a form of 'no' long before he stops talking. I have started to drift away from his speech when he is suddenly talking about my father.

"Your father and I have also discussed it and we agree that's what's best is that we do not mix your portfolio at this stage." he says "The most sensible thing to do would be to take Physics. It compliments the other two sciences well and employers will see it as a strong foundation. It will be familiar to them."

He stops talking. I get the sense that my feet are swinging again so I shift in my chair and uncross them. I do not know what to say. I can feel the moment though, in my chest and I know I need to say something.

"But I enjoy English" I say and even before I have finished saying it I feel a flush of shame. It is not an argument, a counter proposal. It is not the response of an adult and I feel reduced by it, pushed down into this small chair.

Mr Hardy's silhouette twitches its head back slightly.

"I'm not rearranging the whole timetable for you. We pride ourselves in our sciences and their timetable has to accommodate the majority of students who have chosen sensibly" he says. He stays still in his chair, looking at me. From outside there is a passing river of shouts and conversation of students heading home, heading off into the late afternoon.

"So we'll put you down as Physics" he says, leaning forward to make a mark on the paper in front of him. I sense it is a tick, a confirmation of something he has written before our meeting.

"OK" he adds after a brief pause. It is not a question. I still do not know what to say, how to recover the conversation back from where he now takes it which is all about an ending. He talks about the swimming team, the football team, the end of semester but he is ushering me from the room and so I leave, stepping out from the narrow half-light, out into the hall and then the day itself. Above the swifts are crying into the softening light.

CHAPTER 5
THE LAKES

"You know his wife left him last year?" says Sash. It is the first thing she says when I tell her about my meeting with Mr Hardy. "Apparently she couldn't take the boredom any more, or so my mum says."

We are sitting on a bench in a small garden tucked away near the centre of our town, too small to call a park, too hidden to call public. Sash rests her coffee cup on her knee and is looking up toward the line the of trees that follow the top of the nearest hill.

"He's a bastard." she says "We know that. But he is sort of right though."

I am not upset by this. I know it to be true really, this world is set up in certain ways and I have in recent years sensed the expectation that we all travel down them, that to try other paths is to create work only for yourself. Sash is just saying what we are discovering.

"What do you want to do?" she says and for a short moment I think she's asking about our plans for the morning, that she too has moved on. I say I don't know and shrug. It is a universal response, a safe response and also the truth. We sit for a few moments and drink our coffee.

"Come on" Sash says, "Let's go for a ride to the lakes."

The lakes are hidden down one of the many folds in this land, behind a non descriptive gate with a faded 'Private' sign.

Though it is locked with a hefty, rusty chain there is no fence on one side, only the undergrowth pressing close. We push through easily and ride up the rough lane into the dimness of the trees. The track is two ruts and gradually the dips and rising tufts of tough grass mean we need to walk.

The first lake is small, fat and round, the trees reaching across its edges. Nothing moves and we carry on down the path, I know it is not the lakes we have come to see, it is the shell of the house that Sash is gently guiding us towards. As we pass the next lake, larger, more confident in its stretch up the narrow valley, something flusters out of its edges under the dipping branch of a tree, a fish or a bird disturbed by our passing. The lakes were once used by anglers, dotted and hunched here and there on small bare curves of shore. Over recent years few come to fish and we see no-one today. There are five lakes, each larger than the last and after these, the house. It sits at what should be a gentle rise of lawn from the blunt end of the largest lake but is now creeping woodland, young, the trees stepping closer to the stone walls each year. The house was never built, never occupied, its construction abandoned, some family history no doubt taking another turn away from such gestures. Only its soft stone outer walls remain, each window ornately fringed with embellishments never seen. Ivy embraces its southern end. In the empty space of its most northern room a sapling is framed by the large window.

Sash has always been fascinated by the house. She told me once that it is not the emptiness of it that interests her but that the emptiness has never left it, that the place has never known anything else. It is not a gloomy place, the soft press of forest on its walls and the light of the passing morning give it a sense of peace, of waiting.

We lean our bikes against the nearest wall and step through the wide doorway into its empty, inner space.

'Its weird to think this place was never lived in" Sash says. She says this every time "All the work then … just abandoned."

The house is well known locally by people who have lived around these tucks and folds in the land, by people in the nearby town. I only know that it was started by a wealthy son before the first world war and never finished, the war tearing its way through the family as much as it tore through many others. I do not know why it is has stood untouched ever since. There is a sense of an untold, incomplete story about the place, as the trees and the bramble draw themselves around the stones.

We stand in the middle of the empty space, where there is a clearing among the rough undergrowth. The dark scorching of ash on bare earth marks where others have been before, their fire long faded and cold. The sun reaches through here. Sash un-shoulders her pack and sits on a nearby stone, it has either tumbled from a wall or was never lifted, never placed.

"Lunch?" she says and we settle to eat amongst the passing of gentle mayflies and the smooth, hushing hum of the woods and the lakes.

Sash wanders off to the lake and I stay with our rucksacks. I have managed to lie quite comfortably with my head resting on one of them, my cap pulled over my eyes and I sink into a half-waking stillness as the warmth of the early afternoon creeps to me over the high walls of the house. There is a tick-tick of a bird somewhere. I feel a sense of lightness, there is nothing for me to do, no-one needs anything from me and, for the first time in the last few days, that constant flicking and jabbing of thoughts about college, Mr Hardy, the sense of a subtle wrong not righted, it fades and my mind puts down the worry beads it has been fumbling.

There is a noise, a soft shifting in the undergrowth somewhere being my head, like something gently settling or rolling amongst the wild blackberry. The edges of my senses sharpen as I listen more intently. It happens again, not the purposeful noise of an animal or the quick, bright flicker of a bird but a small collapse of something pushing into the tangle of bracken.

I sit up. The noise is coming from a dim corner of the house, where the outer wall is joined by a half built inner wall. I strain to listen and think I can hear the settling of branches still supple with new growth recently disturbed. Briefly I look towards where the lake lies hidden beyond the high front wall. There is no sign of Sash.

I get up carefully and push through the brushing leaves of the bracken, lifting the arcing, catching spines of bramble and eager hawthorn away. My movement throws into the air brittle bursts of noise, the enclosure wrapping them around everything, holding them. In the dim corner there is a structure, low to the ground, it sits in the angle of the two walls. The undergrowth blurs its edges and it is not until I push closer that I see that it is an opening, a stone framing of rough steps leading into darkness. A teasing pull towards it runs up my neck, a sense of something unexplored drawing me in though I hesitate, the thought of going underneath holding me away. Eventually I teeter over the edge of my fear and, pushing aside the thorny brambles I step down into the coolness of the earth.

The dark is not complete, there is a subtle light, it seems to pulse from the rough stones that line the passage and wash gently at the uneven steps. I instinctively reach out to steady myself against the wall, the stones are dry, their roughness fills the contours of my hand. All sound stops except for the flat, scraping of my footsteps. The steps are uneven but they have a certainty of purpose, to carry me down into the soft dark. I stop, turn back to look towards the entrance. The passage must have curved, or the ceiling has dipped, I cannot see the light of the day I have left behind though there is still enough around me to carry on, feeling the rise of the unknown in my throat.

My foot feels the bottom of the stairs before my eyes see it, the sound and solidity of the stone announcing it. There is a rough passage curving gently away from me. Again I stop, there are instincts playing across my breathing, asking me to turn around but the light, this soft light, does something to the dark, holds it away from smothering me and I step further into it. The stones of the walls are ordered, laid one upon the other purposely though the floor feels much more of the earth, uneven stone and hard soil. The air is still, cool, my passing the only movement. I go deeper now and I notice the walls begin to lose their crafting, here and there larger sections of rock, older, unmoving, are pushing through, breaking up the smaller, stuttering lines until eventually the constructed walls fade and I am surrounded by raw stone, the huge press of it making my heart sound in my ears until I have to stop and force the air out of me, taking in a longer, slightly ragged breath until the beating pulse in my head settles enough for me to move on.

The ceiling dips ahead and I stoop to pass under it. I do not know whether I am hoping that the passage comes down to a puckering halt of rock, forcing me to turn back, or whether I want it to carry on its knotted way.

I sense water before I hear it. I feel the space before I see it. There is a change in the air around me, a deepening and cooling, a texture that lines my lungs and fills my nose that is old, clean. An outcropping of stone pushes into the passage and I have to place my hands on it to get around. It is dry, cold, the strength of it hard against my palms. On the other side one side of the passage turns away, disappears into a gloom. The ceiling lifts away from me and I am suddenly in a large cavern. There is a flat, still crescent of water sweeping out and away from me. Somewhere the light of the world above has found its way into this place and it strikes down from the high roof, falling at the end of the pool furthest from me. As my eyes adjust, I see a low bar of rock and sand jutting out into the water. It is here that the falling light lands, soaking into the darkness of the earth. It is here that there is a shape, some form, someone sitting on the ground, the arch of its back, the curve of shoulders towards me.

The silence in the cavern is that of a held breath, it is not absolute, somewhere there is the steady drip of water into the flat surface of the pool. I stand at the edge of the sand bar and watch the seated figure. Its face is tucked in, turned towards the floor, covered by an unruly mass of dark hair, struck through with marbling veins of grey. I do not know why I am here, there is a creeping fear climbing my spine, here in the half light, under the earth and the stone, the trees and the sky somewhere else above me. I get a sudden urge to speak, to give some voice to the fear that sits in my chest.

"Who are you?"

The who comes out as a breath, too high. Instead of taking the sound and flinging it around the stone and the water, the cavern smothers it, it becomes flat and quickly seeps away into the sand beneath me.

The figure does not move. Then, at the point I feel the next breath pushing to be taken, its head raises from its chest and the shoulders uncurl. It levers itself up on two long arms, unfolding from the earth until it stands and turns towards me. The light that strikes from the roof above seems to strengthen, the sun above pushing through and it throws the figure into silhouette It is taller than me and though the clothes it is wearing hide its shape, there is a leanness that strikes through, a sense of muscle and bone that has been worn down by time.

The figure stands in front of me. I cannot see its face in the shadows, amongst the long hair, but I can feel it regarding me, assessing me. It raises an arm towards me, a hand of sinew and veins, its palm uppermost, offered to me. I am mere feet away. If I were to reach out I could take that hand in mine, the urge to do so runs like a current down my arm.

The skin is grey with age, mottled through with the twisting blues of veins. It is steady, insistent and I reach out, placing my hand carefully in it. It is cold, I knew it would be but I did not expect the soft pliability of skin that moulds itself to mine. We stand like this while somewhere in the darkness that drip, drip, drip of water.

With a fierceness that seems too sudden, too quick in this place of stillness, it closes its hand around mine, its fingers hard, thrusting between my own and I am held, secured to this strange thing and it leans towards me. I look up, look into its face though it is shrouded in tumbling hair. Cheekbones, a jutting jaw, a sharp nose, I only get a sense of them. I cannot see the eyes, hidden in the shadow of a high brow and hair. A tremor seems to pass through me and the cave is suddenly much colder than I realised.

Then a voice. It comes from the rocks, the high ceiling, the waters of the pool. It comes from this creature.

"This is the time."

It is slate, it is earth, it balances on the edge of whisper and there is both certainty and urgency in it. I feel the grasp of its hand tighten, imagine the sinews and the braided muscles sharpening in the dim light, feel the pull of it, drawing me towards it and I begin to struggle, my legs begin to brace and wake to a call to run. I hear myself begin to say "no", half formed at first then more certain, a half shout rising automatically from my stomach. The air of the cave is still, the waters are still but I want to move and I cannot free myself of that clutching hand. The strike of light from above seems to fade suddenly and I see the figure in front of me become the deeper shadow of the rock. I become cold with fear as I can no longer see the shape of it before me, just that strong and desperate hand still drawing me towards it. The dark washes in, I feel the press of the earth all around me and I close my eyes to shut it out, to preserve the image of the light.

"Dan!"

I hear my name before I see anything. Then, light, soft light all around me. The dry smell of trees, the heavier note of the waters of the lake, then the sounds, the quick crack of the bracken as I sit up but then the limitless sounds of the sky and air above me, the space opening all around me. I feel Sash's hand on my shoulder and I raise my own to gesture to her that I am ok.

Later Sash sits next to me and we watch the surface of the lake, the flat spread of it between the trees. The afternoon light is saturated with the early heat of summer and the cold cries of crows have given way to the high calls of the swifts above the valley.

"This is the time?" Sash says and I nod, "Wow. Or rather … hmmm"

I look at her. She is chewing at a finger, her eyes fixed on the lake. There seemed little point in not telling her what had happened and, anyway, she drew it out of me before my head had fully cleared, even as she guided me gently out of the house to sit by the lake. It was right. I could sense it, right that we both knew, that we were both drawn in. Though Sash did, at first, go through the motions of asking if she needed to get help, both of us knew that was not needed and she accepted my assurance that I was ok, that I just needed to sit here for a bit.

"This is the time. This is the time" she turned it over to herself "What is it the time for then I wonder?"

I only shrug.

"You know there's no stairs back there?" she says and looks at me, "I checked when I got our bags. Just weeds and rubble. And I think someone's used it as a toilet" She pulls a small frown of disgust.

I am not surprised to hear it. The sun has a clear sky and throws itself across my shoulders and out across the wood, the lake. There is an oily film of sweat running fingers down my back.

"That lake looks inviting" Sash says and half laughs and she considers the dark waters, nodding, pushing out her bottom lip as she considers it. There is a small beach of sand and pebbles, possibly a fishing spot, and Sash wades into the lake from it. She looks back happily at me, smiling.

"It'll be .. What's the word … bracing?" she says

We are both young enough to be awkward undressing in front of each other, old enough to be aware of another's naked skin. My own feels so pale amongst all the life of the woods. We stop instinctively when we are both down to our underwear, unsure.

"Look, I'm not riding home in wet pants, so I don't care if you don't?" Sash says and quickly strips, turning her back to me. "Besides, I ain't interested in anything you've got Boy." She quickly walks into the water and fold herself into it, gasping with the shock. Her skin is dark and cool and seems to be familiar with the colours of the wood, the stones and the water.

"Come on you wuss, I won't look!" she calls and turns easily on to her front, swimming out towards the deeper waters.

I hook my thumbs in my pants and quickly pull them off, clambering into the water, my shyness pushing me to sink into the cover of water quickly. It is cold and sharp and I pant with it, though I am immediately smiling and striking out with a quick breast stroke to follow Sash.

"Maybe you're psychic" says Sash. We are floating in the middle of the lake. The water seems warm now and the sky above us has begun to thicken with the late afternoon sun, threads of high cloud running the tilting light towards an evening that waits over the horizon. I murmur some response, unsure whether I like the suggestion.

"It's what I said before … maybe you're being contacted, something needs to tell you something" she says. Though we are floating, we keep moving, the water is deep enough for a chill to reach around our skin.

"Maybe you're just weird" she says, this time with the tailing end of a laugh.

"Right! Enough!" I say and quickly flip on my front to splash her, the green and white arc of it briefly catching the light. Sash screams, ducking under the water, resurfacing quickly and returns my attack with another sheet of water. We fight like this for a while, laughing and shouting. From the nearby trees three crows take flight, their sharp warning calls stutter down the valley.

"Seriously though, what do you think it is?" Sash says. We are drying ourselves in the last strength of the afternoon sun. I offer my t shirt as a towel and look away, down the lake as Sash pats her skin dry next to me.

"I don't know" I say and there is a heavy sigh threaded through it "I thought it might be just dreams but …" I pause. Sash stops drying herself and drapes the damp shirt over one of my shoulders. I am aware of my nakedness but have my back to her.

"But the whole pool thing. And that I found you unconscious?" she says

The crows have returned, their wings cracking against the sides of the valley, amongst the trees.

"Maybe I'm sick?" I say, voicing a fear. There is a soft silence and then Sash lays a hand gently on my shoulder, her cool skin looks full of life against the paleness of my own.

"Do you want to go and see someone?" she says "Just in case?"

I shrug. Sash sits next to me and I feel the heat of her along my arm, my thigh. We sit like this while the day gently turns towards the amber of late afternoon and our skin cools.

"OK, put some clothes on Danny Boy, I'm tired of seeing your pasty, white legs" she says and heads towards her own clothes.

The ride back down the valley seems longer than I remember. At the sagging gate we are back on the arching lane and we cycle easily along the valley bottom, eventually becoming two more figures amongst others in the town.

Chapter 6
Fayre

"Are you going to the 'fayre'?"

It seems an odd text message but its from Sash so its not, the full proper spelling marking her out from some of the others from college; she has always done this, never giving way to abbreviations.

"It wouldn't be right for someone who studies English" she told me once, when I teased her about it, calling her an old girl. She has a point and I noticed I began to do the same, at first just with her and then with others.

Breakfast is nearly finished, just the lukewarm cup of tea cupped in my hand, my brother rattling on about something to mum who is busying herself amongst the cupboards, her hands flashing across the sink. In a gap in his aimless wandering, my mum turns to me and asks "And what are you doing today?"

"Apparently I'm going to a 'fayre'. With Sash" I say, though I hardly look up from cup.

There is a kind of tense waiting that has hung like an unwelcome air around our daily routines, a half held breath that gives all of the brief exchanges between my parents and I these past few weeks a sense of something else, something waiting to break, the oppressive bland heat of a summer's day calling for the storm. We have not mentioned college, nor the letter from Mr Hardy, written to my father and left there on the side next to the fridge.

I have read the letter. Of course I read it, I was supposed to. It talked about how Mr Hardy and I had discussed things 'thoroughly', how I had 'acknowledged' the situation, how he and my father's previous discussions had been 'confirmed'. It talked about my attitude, about my need to focus and apply myself. It referred to a need for me to 'cultivate' and 'broaden' and 'establish an improved social network'. At the bottom, a neat simple form, requiring my signature, asking me to sign under the brief bullet list of three words - biology, chemistry, physics. The date had already been filled out, in the neat even hand of my father.

It loitered now still, the whiteness of it against the wood of the counter and the smudging print of the local paper.

"A fayre?" my brother says, looking at me with the crooked smile of teasing "A fairy fayre?" He snorts. Cornflakes and milk splash from his spoon back into the bowl. My mother cuts it off "Ruth's got a stall there this year" she says, clattering the rack of the dishwasher. "Says she'd give it a try. Last year that new bakery sold out by lunchtime. So she thought she'd give it a go." She pauses and looks out of the window, judging the sky, nodding at the blueness of it "Well, I suppose so. But I'll need your help moving the rabbit feed before you disappear anywhere"

It amazes me that a market town that seems so small, so folded away into these quiet tucks of the land, can hold this many people. Its edges made crooked by the corners of the buildings thrown down where needed, the market square is full of people, the sound of the numerous, seperate conversations hardly rising above the tumbling roofs, gathering in this low well of brick and cobbles. There is enough space to move between them, slowly, politely and I weave through the crowd, heading towards the cafe on the western side, our cafe, the only cafe. Sash is waiting, her blue rucksack on one shoulder, standing against a wall. She is looking away from me, down the street, watching how the flow of people seems to wash from side to side, crossing each other.

"Allright?" I say and she smiles at me, hooking her thumb over one shoulder to point into the cafe, a question that already has an answer. The coffee is hot and strong and we stand in the shade of the old post office watching the square.

"You spoken to your dad yet?" she asks, taking the lid off her cup and blowing gently on her coffee. I shake my head and watch two children run between the legs of the crowd.

"You going to?" It is asked lightly but there seems weight behind it. We have talked about it before.

"Not sure there's much point" I say, "They seem to have decided it's the sciences"

Sash turns her head towards me, very quickly, she takes a quick breath

"Dan, for god's sake …"

Somewhere near the centre of the square there is a loud thumping, four solid beats then a jarring, lifting noise of fiddles, pipes, an accordion. There is a shouting, a calling from those nearest the musicians and then the square itself seems to tip over into a rhythmic melody, its cadence familiar yet spun through with off, clashing harmonies that briefly tangle then trace their own paths away from each other.

Whatever Sash is going to say is lost in a gentle wave of clapping that spreads out from the centre until most people have joined in. I beat my free hand against my thigh and pretend to watch the ceremony, though I can see little over the heads of the people in the square. The insistent thumping of the drum has crept into the cobbles, I feel it in my feet, my shins and every third beat seems to land heavily in my chest. The voices near the market cross are rough, everyday voices now chanting and half singing. Something briefly appears above the heads of the crowd, a dark fluttering, but I do not see it before it dives beneath again. Then, again, it rises and dives, something awkwardly raised and flourished then brought low. There is a movement near it, a recurrence, a rhythmic step and jump as a dance starts up around the musicians like the steady push and swirl of an underground spring breaking into air and light.

Sash is watching now. The frown that had shadowed her face replaced with curiosity. Whatever we needed to say has now gone. There are small eddies in the crowd, people beginning to move, there is something coming towards us, making its way from the centre, across the square. The thump of the drums and the repeating cycle of the chanting voices, the lifting of the music, they are all on the move, making a rocking, tilting progress towards the eastern exit, toward where we are standing. It is like watching something push its way through a restless sea. The flicker and flash of the dancing figure is seen more often now and I sense a form to it, a gaunt shape, throwing long thin arms above the heads of the crowd. They seem to be made of joints and knuckle and though there is a pattern to their movements, there is also a flailing wildness. The crowd push themselves away from it, out of the way of those flashing arms. The singing seems to be all around us now and I try to hear the words but they have been worn smooth by repetition and I can only grasp at a few, the song is full of the light and the dark. There is a brooding sense of the hunt, a chase. It is not clear whether there is hope or fear.

Sash looks at me, grinning broadly at this moment but I suddenly cannot smile. Her eyes flicker from my face to the approaching figure. I feel a sudden sense of recognition crawl from my stomach. The dancing figure is huge, its jointing arms still marking out erratic wild patterns, raising against the light of the sky. It towers over the crowd, a gaunt frame of black rags that snap and crack with each sharp gesture. Its legs are hidden but they too are following some pattern, following a halting stepping routine marked out by the beating of the drums. It arches, unfolds, folds, twists and turns. There is no head, just a curving spine of ragged cloak towards a rough hood. My senses suddenly feel the snow and ice, the sky flickers to the dark, a heavy moon above a hill top. There is no-one now between us. This tumbling thing swings around on one long leg braced against the stones, its arms out, scything through the air, until it faces me. The music reaches a flat, insistent rhythm, each part quickly returning from its own path to join with the others, a single urging beat and then it abruptly stops. The singers and many of the crowd give a long cry, a shout in unison. The dark figure raises its arms to the sky and on the falling note of the shout it lowers them to enfold me in dark rags that smell of frozen earth and snow.

The bass drum thumps, once, twice and then the band and the singers pick up the song again. The wave of it breaks over us both and I am quickly released from the embrace, the figure flicking its ragged arms up and away from me. That insistent beat moves the slowly pacing tangle of dancers and musicians on, into the streets of the town, the press of the onlookers loosens and passes. I stand very still, my heart still pushing at my throat, like the thumping drum that is still knocking at us.

"Dan?" says Sash, her face comes into view and with it I come back into myself. "Are you ok?"

I give a half huff of laughter and look at my feet, trying to shrug it off but there is something about Sash's look that stops my usual turning away and though I don't look at her, I do answer.

"That thing, the tall thing" I say and she looks down the street where the ragged sweep of its arms mark where the crowd is at its tightest knot. "Its what I saw. On the hill, that first time."

Sash nods "Yes. As soon as I … it made me think of … of what you told me."

We stand for a minute, people are ebbing around us. There is just the muted thump of the drum, bouncing from the walls of the houses, giving it an odd, hollow echo.

"Well … so that means we should at least be able to find out what it is." she says and she adjusts the straps on her pack "More coffee. And more to the point, cake?"

I smile and nod. The cafe has a small queue and we stand together not really talking until we are served. The woman who serves us is focused on the act of it, polite enough though in the flow of a busy day and we are soon out in the light again. We head away from the centre and the people fade away as we climb a narrow lane through the wooded hill, heading to the flat expanse of the common ground above the town. The climb is steep though the lane turns and twists back on itself. There is a bench in a gap where younger ash trees have been planted and we sit, drinking our coffee, enjoying the soft sweetness of the cakes. The day has drawn in a thin cover of light cloud, muting the sun though there is little breeze and we are warm from the climb.

"Martin will know" say Sash. She is looking across the valley towards a hazy line of trees. "Sorry, I mean Mr Johns" She places the emphasis on the Mr and slowly rolls her head and eyes towards me.

I can only know him as Mr Johns, using his first name, seeing him as a 'Martin' gives him too much. He is a teacher, our history teacher. If he becomes Martin, he steps outside the college, outside the lecture room and then I have to imagine him in the world, with all the life that comes with it. Sash, however, at some point in the past has already done this with all of our teachers, referring to them by name, even when talking to them. Oddly none of them have ever seemed to mind, even though they refer to themselves by their surnames. Except Mr Hardy - who Sash refers to as Hardy. The sudden thought of him arrives like a deeper cloud and it breaks my train of thought.

"Good idea" I say, though I am unsure about it, unsure whether I want to know. Facing this gives it detail, brings it out from the suggestion of being a dream that could so easily be allowed to fade and places it in the world. I am not sure I want that. I am not sure I ever want such things.

The afternoon brings on a pale veil of cloud drawn in quietly from the south until the whole sky has become muted, the sun smearing towards the horizon. There is a place on the other side of the rough, flat common land that rambles across this hilltop, joining the five valleys that run through this part of the land. There is a soft fold in the edge of the common, a tuck down over the lip of the northernmost valley, where a stand of oak and beech line the gentle sides of a small hollow. Sash and I are sitting with our backs against an oak tree, our bikes tangled together nearby.

"Maybe you're supposed to do something." she says "Perhaps its a call. A sign. Maybe you're the Chosen One!" she laughs and I can't help smiling.

"Sure. I'm special. I've been chosen from amongst all these people to … to do something. Save the world."

She picks a leaf from the ground and turns it in her hands.

"Yeah sure, you're a god" she says, "No … I meant maybe you're being told something important here. I don't know. Even if, lets say, its all in your head, it could still be that somewhere, deep inside, you know there's something you need to do. Or say. And your brain … that part of you … that real … the real you is trying to get your attention."

In the pause that follows, the distant drone of a plane fills the afternoon with heaviness. I don't say anything, although I am listening, and my breath has become a shallowness in my chest. Sash is frowning delicately now, concentrating on the leaf.

"My mum says that her family used to talk about the old one that's always inside you. A sort of you that has existed long before this version of you" she says and she strokes the edges of the leaf, "And this old one knows what it needs, has a sort of wisdom about things. If we can learn to talk to it, there inside us, we can hear its wisdom."

"You mean like a soul?"

"Maybe, though my mum has never used that word. The problem is … sometimes we don't listen. Or sometimes we don't even know the old one even exists and we are doing something or about to do something that it knows, it understands is not, well, not right. It has to tell you, has to try and let you know somehow."

Sash stops. She has been looking down through the trees. We can see the small fields and copses of the lower valley through the gaps in the trees, their stone walls making erratic boundaries. The other side of the valley is not as high and beyond the land settles into a gentle swell, fading away from us.

"That creature, that thing" I say "In the square. That's not my soul." I try and keep it as a statement but cannot avoid the upward tilt of the question.

"Hmm. Could be though" she says, "Its certainly ugly enough" Sash smiles directly at me and I 'hey!" at her, punching at her shoulder in mock indignation.

We push our bikes up out of this quiet hollow, back out onto the expanse of the common. The day has passed over and there is a sense of movement in everything.

Chapter 7
Mr Johns

"Ah yes, the Soul-Less Man" says Mr Johns and he turns to his laptop, tilting his head back to look through the bottom of his lenses "The Old Man or, as he was once known, The Catcher."

The class room is dim with the dullness of the day, the light pale and even. The large windows are speckled with recent rain, the droplets clinging in the corners, along the bottom edge. Nothing moves outside, not the sky nor the trees, nor the high hedge that marks the edge of the playing fields.

"Here we are." he turns his laptop towards us, "Actually I can get it up on the screen, hang on"

It fades into a cold, blue square of light then, with the merest of flickers there is the creature, a black ink drawing of it, the limbs high above the head, the joints appearing numerous, disorganised. The artist has chosen to draw it with its back towards us and there is no face, just the suggestion of a hooded head. The body is wrapped in dark rags, their frayed ends curling out in all directions as if blown by many twisting winds. Crouched before it, arms held tightly over her head, is a woman, her face full of terror.

"It's uncertain where the story originates from" Mr Johns settles into his lecture. There is just Sash and me, the rest of the class has left. It was Sash's idea to stay behind and ask. She asked with a light touch, a curious note to the end of her sentences, explaining that we had seen the figure during the fayre, even adding in the detail of it catching me, smiling at me, drawing Mr Johns into the gentle teasing.

"It could be an old local folk tale, its origins lost now. Or it could be a more recent invention. Well, I say recent, but I mean eighteenth or mid nineteenth century even. A sort of bogey man invented by the local industrialists and land owners to keep the folk in line."

"What's it doing?" says Sash. She steps closer to the screen and studies the cowering woman.

"Well, the stories vary of course but the common element is that the Catcher seeks out those who have somehow become lost, strayed from the path - whatever was accepted as the path at the time. He … or it … takes their soul as its own, not having one, you see. I suspect the thinking is that if a person is not going to use it, it can somehow."

Sash is quite still.

"Is she black?" she says and Mr Johns and I study the cowering women more closely.

"Hmm, yes, I think she is" says Mr Johns, "That gives this a rather more sinister interpretation doesn't it."

They both study the picture. Outside the last students are passing, their conversation streaming around each other, indistinct as the soft birdcalls over the trees beyond.

"I've not heard or seen the Catcher anywhere else, is it just a local thing?" I ask.

"Oh yes, quite local" Mr Johns says, he taps the laptop and another picture appears, a photograph this time. It is the town square, full of people gathered around the market cross and there in the middle of them is the gaunt form of the Catcher. Though the photograph is in colour, they seem dull, roughly daubed. The faces of the people are too yellow, here and there the burnt reds of a neckerchief or a skirt.

"Ah, one from my own past here. My father took this in 1973." Mr Johns smiles, "I'm there, look…" he points to a pale child, holding the hand of a thin women near the edge of the crowd, his legs white against the brown shorts and sandals. "Not sure the hairstyle has changed much." He laughs at himself gently.

"Is there anything in the local stories about how to avoid it?" Sash asks, her face serious. She has not taken her eyes from the screen, studying the smiling faces there standing underneath that dark, tall figure "I mean, what do you do if you know its coming after it?"

Mr Johns lifts his shoulders, his head back and up, he draws his lips down, the lower one pushing out against the upper and then releases it all with a soft sigh. "Well, you mean other than run like … er … like a fast thing?" Sash and I nod at the same time and there must be something in it that makes Mr Johns halt the forming of his smile. He studies us both briefly and then turns back to the laptop. "Good question actually. Always good to ask what happens beyond the main story. I recall there is something on this. Lets have a look" He studies the laptop, unaware that it is also being projected on the screen behind him. He is looking through a list of files. He finds one and double-clicks. A plain, typed document appears on the screen, even justified paragraphs.

"This is a transcription from an older book - think its in the local archives still. Its 1923 but it does refer to an older piece about the Old Man and I think …" he scans through the text, hunching forward, his eyes made small with concentration, "Yes, here it is … 'There is a less substantiated tale about a man, a local farmer, who, having been chased by the Old Man over a manner of days and nights, sold his farm rather quickly, moving from the valley. The story seems to have been retained in the local lore if only to note the incredulity this action - taken by one from an old farming family of good reputation. Though the detail is lacking, it does appear to indicate that this man established himself near Swindon, living out an unremarkable life with a new family.'"

Mr John sits back, places his hand on his thighs. Somewhere, coming from the open window, there is a fresh smell of rain on the air. The light has dimmed and the afternoon has faded further into the greys and greens of the sky and earth.

"Well, there you go … that could mean a number of things couldn't it?" Mr Johns says. I sense he is talking more to himself than us.

"But he got away. That's probably good" says Sash.

"Probably good" Mr Johns, as if realising there are students with him, looks up and smiles then nods at the windows. The rain is uncertain against them, hard drops, infrequent, they appear suddenly on the glass and hold themselves there motionless. "I'd better let you two go then" and he closes the laptop, reaching for his rucksack under the table.

Outside the rain is not enough to bother me, though I walk my bike for a while, enjoying the moment. Sash has ridden away though as she swung her bike around and stood hard on the pedals she said "There you go then … just move to Swindon!" I smile and pretend to throw something at her but she does not see this, she is already down the drive. And what I want to say, I don't, that the farmer gave it all up, gave something away. The afternoon seems to have settled into this indecisive, forgettable place between rain and sun.

CHAPTER 8
CHASE

It is raining. The sides of the tent have become a constant machinery of raindrops, pushing away our conversation, pushing us towards ourselves and long moments of listening to it all around us. In amongst the steady beating of the rain, the heavier thump of larger drops falling from the trees sound as a loud erratic drum. The effect should be calming but instead it teases at my nerves, fills my head with the sense of being trapped in this small space.

Sash is picking at the edge of the blanket drawn around her shoulders, the rain suggesting the need for it despite the warmth of the evening. Summer has raised itself across the landscape and the trees, fields, the hedgerows and gardens are saturated with it, brimming with its full force. Today's rain arrived quietly under cover of a few hours of sultry cloud and after several bright, hard days of light and heat the earth drinks it quickly down. Suddenly the air is full of the taste of soil, of stone and leaf.

We abandoned any idea of a campfire and quickly settled into the tent, using its small porch to heat beans, lightly toast bread. We had wine, lifted quietly from Sash's kitchen. It was rough and raw and filled us with that first flush of warmth.

"How's it going with Amber?" I ask, there is a pause, an easing in the rain. Sash nods, pushing out her bottom lip slightly. I think she is trying to treat it as any other conversation though I notice her eyes ease into a smile, the sides of her mouth arc gently.

"Good thanks" she says, "Early days, you know, so we're just …" she shrugs and looks at me, smiling fully now.

"That's good." I say. It feels not enough. There is another conversation behind this one, not difficult, just real. I smile back at her and she lets out a quick sigh of laughter through her nose, looking away, looking out of the tent doorway down the slope of the field towards another line of trees.

I drink wine from my mug and keep smiling at her. The warmth of the evening begins to seep back through the rain. The breeze that had curled up the gentle slope of the meadow has died away now and the summer's night begins to grasp at everything, stilling the branches, the leaves, the grasses around us.

"Is it good?" I say, still smiling. Though Sash and I have known each other for some years, this territory of other people is new to us.

"Fuck off Boy" she emphasises the Boy as usual, but she is smiling and we both laugh "I'm not fuelling your mucky boy fantasies." She flips the blanket back from her shoulders and reaches for the bottle. I laugh.

The rain has passed over and we are left with that ponderous slow drum of water dropping from the branches above us.

"Well, I hope it is" I say, feeling the words in my mouth as they form "Good, that is. I hope its good."

Sash looks at me and nods.

We don't bother with a fire though we do sit outside. The light has gone now but the darkness is not complete despite the cloud cover, despite the trees at our backs. There are broad shapes, sweeps of dark and grey all around us. We sit and take it in.

"Have you thought about what you're going to do?" Sash says, her voice is plain, simple in the dark "About next term, your choices. Your life I guess."

I shake my head, though its a lie, there is constant liturgy of it in my thoughts all the time now, there in the background, turning over the same questions obsessively.

"No" I say "Not really. I don't know."

From the trees that run along the shallow fold in these hills there is a piercing shriek, an owl. It makes both of us jump and for a time we listen to the slicing sharpness of it, out there in the night.

The rain returns, it pushes away any conversation and we settle against the hard ground to sleep. I lay listening to the hammering against the thin fabric, a solid sound, constant, the dark air is saturated with it. I know Sash is awake, I sense her presence next to me though neither of us speak or move, just lay there listening to the world pass over us. I do not know what time it is, just that I have slept briefly as the rain squalled along the the field. The sleeping bag is warm and despite the hardness of the ground I hover in a half waking state.

There is a sharp screech, it strikes its way between the beating raindrops and cracks around me. I jump, my legs twitching, my stomach fluttering, my eyes opening wide. In the dark there is nothing, no sense of shock, just absence. The sound of the rain is solid, unwavering. The screech comes again, piercing and stark, the storm cannot mute it.

Sash turns slowly, I feel her next to me, can sense her head lifting to listen. Another screech, this time it seems to tail away, ending more plaintively, less certain.

"Can you hear that?" says Sash, her voice caught somewhere between a whisper and pushing above the rain.

I nod, then realise neither of us can see so say yes. Sash sits up, I hear the rustle of it.

"Its got to be the owl again." I say, though the uncertainty of it turns it into a question. Sash waits, listening.

"Do owls hunt in the rain?" she says

Another screech fills the night, this time closer, wrapping the tent with its cold brittle edges. We both jump. I feel the warmth of Sash's shoulder on my arm, we have edged closer to each other. I begin to feel around for my head torch but stop. The idea of sudden light in the night somehow scares me, an announcement of us here in the corner of this small field.

Another cry fills the night, it has a harshness about its edges, a raw note threaded through it, pain, desolation.

"That's closer." I say. I have unconsciously reached for my shirt, pulling it slowly on.

"That's no owl" says Sash and I feel her quick movement as she pushes herself out of her bag. We are pulling on clothes hurriedly, an unspoken plan, the act of it suggesting flight or preparation to face something as yet unseen. When I hear the rustle of Sash's anorak, I realise that we are leaving the tent, I understand that this is what I too need to do, to be outside and not confined. I pull my jacket on as Sash zips the door.

We are both hurrying now. The laces of my shoes seem strange and I fumble my way through tying them. Sash is outside when the next screech fills the air. It is all around us this time, so loud that I duck instinctively, so near that I turn my head towards the darkness out in the field.

"Oh god" I hear Sash say "There's something in the field."

In amongst the steady sluicing of the rain there is another noise, a slow ripping of something passing through wet grass, pushing its way across the sodden field.

The next cry is so loud I cover my ears instinctively and start running towards the edge of trees behind us. Sash is just ahead of me. We scramble over the wall and plunge into the wet darkness of the trees.

The land is full of rain. The ground is slippery with it, my legs soon become cold, wet and my footing unsure. We are both crashing through the undergrowth, the night full of our noise. Sash is still in front of me, the branches whip back at me as she pushes ahead. A piercing scream behind us, raw and close. Neither of us react though our flight through the trees becomes more ragged. There is a low wall at the edge of the trees. It marks out a lane that follows the line of trees. In the dark it looks like a black river, the night runs along it. Sash is already pulling herself across the wall when the next scream strikes through darkness behind us. I scramble over the stones, their harsh cold grabbing at my hands and thighs. An unruly hedge runs along the other side of the lane. We can only go left or right now and even in our flight the decision stops us, I can hear Sash breathing hard and then her hand is on my arm in the dark.

"That way" she says, a half whisper, she points right.

"Shh, wait, wait" I say "Listen"

We stand there in the lane and listen to the trees. The rain has lessened and the noise of it has fallen away. There is nothing, no noise just the night around us.

"Nothing" Sash says "I can't hear anything"

I nod in the dark.

"What is it? Where is it?" she says

The next scream, when it comes, is so loud it knocks against my teeth, pushes through my stomach and fills the night so completely that for a moment I think there is nothing else in the world but that rending, tearing noise. It seems to come from above us, behind us, within us. Sash screams and I hear myself joining in.

"Run!" I shout and we both take off down the lane, towards the sharp slope of the hillside into town.

There is a bus stop, a stone shelter and rough bench as the first row of houses mark the edge of the town. We stop running and sit in the dimness of its dank interior. Street lights have filled the night with their cold, constant brush of half light. The edges of the world emerge from the night again. We sit, breathing heavily. Both of us keep looking back up the lane, not knowing what to see there. Then Sash laughs, a breathless laugh caught between deeper gasps. I find myself joining in and we sit like this for a few minutes, looking at each other but also looking out into the dark, up the hill.

"Your dad's going to kill you" she says, "If we don't get that tent."

We laugh again. I lean back against the stonework, my breathing steadying. I am nodding and smiling but the sweat that I feel running into the small of my back is beginning to cool.

"What the fuck was that?" Sash says eventually

I don't want to answer because naming it must either put a lie to it or, worse, create a truth that hovers around us unspoken. I just shake my head.

"We both heard it though" I say, "I mean, it wasn't just me."

It is a question. Sash hears it, I see her nod and it is like being confirmed in a long held truth. My throat tightens and I feel tears. I look away, back out into the half light at the edge of town.

We sit there, not really knowing what to do next. The rain returns, less certain now, just enough to cool the air and this, combined with the drying sweat on my skin makes me feel cold and I start to hunch, wrapping my arms around myself.

"Come on" Sash says, "We can't stay here all night. We can go back to my house. Mum's on a night shift."

I look at her.

"Or we can go back to the tent?" she says and raises her eyebrows at me. She reads my face and says "OK, back to mine. We can go and get the stuff in the morning. When its light."

We step out into the gentle rain and half jog deeper into town. As we turn into Sash's lane there is a short, piercing shriek from the dark at the end of her lane. I stop, my breath stops.

"An owl" Sash says, though her eyes are wide, " Definitely an owl."

We hurry to her house.

Chapter 9
Back in the Cafe

The hiss of the coffee machine makes me jump. Sash looks across her mug at me, a sort of knowing lightness in her eyes.

"At least the tent was ok" she says.

The cafe is not full and we are sitting in a window seat. Two women, both with small children, have spread themselves in one corner. An older woman sits by herself at one of the tables along the other wall, her hands neat on the table, she looks out into the town square.

In our rush last night we did not close the tent. Inside was covered in a fine dampness, our sleeping bags cold to the touch. Folding them, pushing the tent into its bag, it felt wrong, the wet slide of it across my hands. While we packed our gear, neither of us spoke. In the light the meadow was filled with summer, the sun had already dried the tops of the grasses, the wild flowers were bright and full. It was only as we took a final look around our camping area, checking we had gathered everything, that I found myself inspecting the longer grass further down the slope, uncertain what I was looking for. Sash saw where I was looking and walked out into the meadow, standing with her hands on her hips, surveying around her.

"Anything?" she said.

"No, nothing, no tracks."

I expected to feel relieved, but I felt frustrated. Surely, something, anything.

"But … but …" I said, and made an exaggerated frown of concern.

"Yeah, I know. We're idiots." it was said lightly, "Hang on, what's this?"

Sash bent down, inspecting something in the grass, reaching in amongst the clover, "Its … its … a piece of the monster!" and she sharply flung something small and dark at me. I ducked, my heart hammering suddenly, my legs starting to push towards the lane again. Something soft and wet hit me on my arm and I heard Sash give a shout of laughter. It was soil, dark and fresh and I stopped, looking at her with my eyes wide, then I laughed, bending to scoop my own handful of earth, saying something like "Oh, you … Right!". Sash gave a delighted squeal and ran towards our bikes. My aim was poor. The light poured around us and the night, the rain was gone. Just for a moment, as I waited for her to finish getting on her bike, I saw the dark earth under my fingernails and, lifting them, I could smell the deeper scent of it. A quick ripple of cold washed down my back but Sash had set off down the lane and I quickly followed.

"Do you think we are idiots then?" I ask. In the light and noise of the cafe the conversation seems easier, more distant. Sash is swirling her coffee in her mug, watching it and she does not answer immediately.

"No" she says, "Not really. There was something."

I watch her. One of the children has wandered towards our table, precarious new steps. His mother does not stop talking to her friend but bends sideways to catch his hand and he stops, watching us with a shy smile. Sash smiles back.

"I don't know though" she says, still watching the boy, "Before you ask. I don't know what it was … is" She looks back at me and I do not know whether her smile is still for the child or has been formed new for me.

"It's the Chaser." I say, trying to adopt a dramatic, hushed tone, drawing out the name.

"That's just convenient. I mean, that could just be us connecting entirely separate things. A chat with Mr Johns, your .. er … dream things. Whatever spooked us …"

The boy has turned his attention to the woman at the other table but she is too engrossed in reading something on her tablet and his smile weakens and he turns carefully back towards his mother, who has kept her hand in his.

"I mean it could have been a cow" Sash says, "Or a sheep. Or a big owl, a really big owl, the mother of all owls. I don't know." Her mug is nearly empty and she is playing with the froth coating its sides, scraping with her teaspoon and letting it drip back into the cup.

"A cow." I say, "We picked a field with no animals. I didn't want to wake up with some smelly thing farting over me, remember?"

She looks up quickly at me.

"Oh don't tempt me Dan, don't make me say it."

We both laugh and she slumps back in her seat.

"Well, then, I don't know. I don't know about things that go bump in the night."

"Or shriek."

"Yeah, or shriek. I mean …" she hesitates and looks out the window, across the square, "OK, I suppose I do think there's stuff we don't know about, that there's more to all this than we know" she raises her chin to take in the square, the cafe, us "But its got to have some reason. If such things do happen, they need to have a reason. It can't be that some random … thing from the unseen world just comes at us, two kids camping in a field."

The coffee machine bursts into its short song of steam and we wait as it eventually fades away. I want to ask why, out loud, bringing what has been tumbling in my head for days into this real world of tables, coffee, mums, Sash.

"What did Mr Jones say about the Chaser?" I ask, more to myself, "That it comes after people who've strayed from the path. Wants their soul." I am half embarrassed, the words, the conversation not one I've ever had. The way the world might work has never occupied a natural place in any of our conversations, we rarely discuss anything beyond this town, these valleys, the many brief stories of school and college that have a such a short, bright intensity while they last.

Sash looks at me, sharp and with such a quick, bright questioning that I halt. There is a brief gap where neither of us seem to take a breath.

"This had better not be about me" she says, evenly. For a moment my thoughts tumble as I try to understand her. Then I sense something beyond the two of us and in it the opening out of her life beyond our time spent in idle escape into the surrounding hills and woods, beyond the usual routine of college days. A sense of her outside all these moments, her family, her other friendships. There is a sudden awareness of space, of opening, it halts my words on the back of my tongue. I take a drink from my mug, it is mostly froth but the act seems to anchor me to this cafe, here in this square.

"I wasn't thinking about you … I mean … not that I … if you want to talk, its …" I say and my words thin out. I feel a warmth in my face, flushing down the sides of my neck.

Sash smiles then, a small smile that just moulds her lips, the corner of her eyes..

"I know" she says "Sorry … Its not about me, not this." Sash keeps her eyes on me until I glance back at her and we both give a brief, gentle laugh. She puts her mug down and begins to run one finger around the rim of it, tilting her head "What do you think its about then?"

I shrug though in the act of it I immediately feel it is wrong, that it too easily pushes away the moment. Sash gives a slight shake of her head, looking at me, her finger paused in its circling.

"Dan," she says, and there is a gentleness in it, though I cannot tell whether it is a giving up or a reaching out "Can I tell you what I think? For what its worth?"

I nod. I look at her, it feels strange, I realise then how many of our conversations, our times together have been spent looking out at the world. Her eyes are light brown. I have not noticed this before.

"Ok, well, I think this stuff you're going through, with your dad and school and all that. Its probably more important than you think. I know its important to you, I can see it. But I think its something beyond you."

The door to the cafe opens with a clatter just as the local bus rumbles across the square. A man comes in, taking a neat backpack from his shoulder, it catches on the corner of the nearest table, rattling it briefly. He mouths sorry to no-one in particular, his eyes already on the chalkboard menu above the serving bar.

"A couple of christmases ago, my grandma was over, staying with us" Sash says "I think she was somewhere in her 80s then. Mum said it was just as she was showing the early signs of slipping away. But I remember her sitting there, in the corner of our lounge watching us all moving around her, watching us all day. I mean we didn't ignore her, but she sat so still, just watching and nodding when we spoke to her. After dinner, mum asked me to check whether she wanted a cup of tea or something, so I took her one and she was there, by herself, and I guess I felt I should stay and talk. I don't know how we got onto it but she began talking about home, about life there. I just listened. I'd not really heard much about her life, or my mum's early life, so it was interesting. I remember perching awkwardly on the arm of her chair, leaning in to hear her better."

Sash pauses, looks out of the window.

"Anyway, towards the end, the gaps between her sentences grew longer and I guess I felt I needed to fill them with something so I said how much I loved hearing her stories, that she seemed full of them. She nodded, placed her hand on mine, patting it and said something odd, a bit quietly. She said that the old stories are still around us, in the land, in places. Its just that we've forgotten many of them. And that we mustn't fall out of our stories, that they keep all the worlds with us."

Sash looks at me "All the worlds. It was such an odd phrase."

We sit, the cafe continues around us. The woman on the next table is gathering herself into her small rucksack and it is her preparations that seem to tip the moment into one of leaving. "Shall we go?" Sash says and she takes her hoody from the back of the chair. We step into the muted sunlight of the square, a high, even cover of cloud loosening the light. It is warm, I feel it on the back of my neck as we head up towards Sash's road.

"You know, you're funny when we get near talking about anything important" she says. She is pulling grass from the side of the lane and weaving the short stalks between her fingers,

"You know its ok to ask. I'm happy to talk about it, my stuff I mean."

I nod.

"I don't mind. Seriously." Her voice is light, the words thrown away, "Although I can't say I'm an expert. Only what I know about myself, who I like. Or about my family and what they've told me about our past, where we come from."

I nod again and Sash laughs at me.

"Doing a grand job there Dan, talking about stuff."

I laugh at this.

"Sure Sash, Ok. I just don't know whether it needs talking about. I mean I don't think its ever been much of a thing with me. I don't mean its not important, just I've never really had any questions, not questioned it."

"Typical boy" she says and throws a knot of grass at me. The air catches it before it reaches me and it falls gently to the tarmac, "Sometimes its not all about you, sometimes other people want to talk. About themselves."

The moment seems to crack like a breaking summer storm. We both laugh and Sash shakes her head. I can feel heat in my face. We are at the foot of Sash's short drive. There is a car, its engine still ticking as it cools.

"Mum's back from work."

We agree to meet up later. Our plan for the evening is a barbecue, up on one of the ridges that look out over the flatter lands towards the distant estuary. I turn towards the lane, heading further up the valley towards my house.

CHAPTER 10
BEACH

I am sitting with my back against a tree, one of the larger oaks at the edge of a line that runs along the sharp ridge that marks the most south westerly edge of this undulating landscape of valleys and hills. The day is hot, so hot that the horizon has blurred with the heat rising from the lands below, flat, marked by the loops of the river coming out of the north east, pushing its way through the fields and thin villages, towards the coast. I have been to this spot before, this tree. On a cooler day, there on the horizon, is the darker line of the sea, caught between earth and sky. Today, just a haze, the edges of the land gently smeared.

It would be wrong to call it an argument, it was as if all of the hidden lines between us had been pulled, were suddenly taut, restraining us, holding my family still, not slipping into the more dangerous currents of argument, of emotion. My father tapping the letter from the college, telling me in that voice that is meant to convey reason, rationality, a voice for some unseen audience, as if the world is watching. My mother, standing near the sink, silhouetted against the morning's bright light, her hands still for once, paying attention, playing her part by not playing any part. My brother, looking only at his breakfast, his hair still rough against his forehead, occasionally flicking his eyes to me, checking, watching. I play my part, my hands cupped around my tea, looking only at the cabinets behind my father.

His speech is not long. He is disappointed - the only word that gets close to any emotion - the rest is about how it will be, how he has decided. He continues to hold the letter that has Mr Hardy's neat, even signature at the bottom. My father selects from it words and phrases, offers them to me as if they have come uninvited into his world, unwelcome, holding them up to show me. Once these words have been laid out in the space between us, I hear how we will all move on, how I will buckle down at the end of the summer. His words are crisper now, there are small spaces between them where nothing else is invited. He tells me that one day I will be grateful. Not today though, it is implied, today I am the disappointing son. I say little, am not expected to and though I consciously say nothing, unwilling to give any sign of agreement, it feels weak, small. Eventually the words are gathered back in and my father leaves the kitchen. My mother and brother watch me, expecting something more from me but I say nothing, and I take my bike and head out into the heat, quickly heading up the lanes, up the hills, wanting height.

The smell of the woodsmoke is out of place amongst the paling heat of this summer's day. It speaks of autumn, of the browning of the year. I open my eyes, disturbed from the retelling. The flatlands and the river spread out before me, the land beginning to turn towards the purples and blues of the evening. From this height everything appears still. The endless teeming of life will be weaved through it all, in the meadows, through the hedges and trees, in each cluster of houses hidden here and there. The river's smooth, continuous line will be drawing towards a sea but, from here, it stands still, a thread lying across the land.

The smell of smoke has strengthened, it fills my sinuses though I do not see any smudging of the air, no darkening of the light to tell me where it might be coming from. I sit forward and look along the ridge to the south. There is something faint, just on the edge of my hearing, a familiar soft crackling of burning wood, lively and nimble, it has the lightness of a small fire. It seems to be coming from behind one of the larger oaks. I wonder who else has found this spot, my spot, feeling a quick flash of irritation. I sit for a while, listening, uncertain whether to announce my presence by moving, There is a sudden crack as of a larger branch splitting in the heat. It makes me jump. The sound of it deepens and there begins a more insistent note, buried under the crackling, the early roar of a fire taking hold, taking its place. It makes me get up, worried now that this may not be a simple campfire.

As I approach the oak, the burning smell fills the whole world, the evening has been pushed aside by it. There is still no sign of smoke though the air does feel thicker around me, catching on my skin and in my hair. The roaring noise is constant now, it has wrapped itself around the lighter snaps of the kindling flames and sounds out its confident note. I lay my hand on the tree in order to peer around it and I feel heat, it thrills along my arm and I instinctively snatch my hand away. There is no campfire, no bonfire in the woods beyond the tree yet the sound of it fills my head, I step around the trunk and quickly the roar of the burning becomes bright and loud. The broad trunk is split, an opening that stretches from the earth to head height. In the opening, a fierce fire burns twisting and pulsing, the flames grasping at its edges. There is heat, smothering at my face, pushing at my t shirt and I take a step back. For a moment I do not know what to do, I stand there in uncertainty. Another fierce crack jolts me and it is as I begin to move back to where my rucksack is propped against another tree, to where my phone is, that I notice the oak is not changing, it is not burning. The flames run themselves across the edges of the opening, across the bark but there is no damage, no blackening or slow shrinking into ash. The fire's ferocity seems to be unimportant to the tree and it embraces it as it embraces the air and the daylight.

I step towards the burning tree and see that there is still an opening in its trunk despite its flames. There is heat but it is the heat of a sun, constant and broad on my face and I stoop a little towards it, trying to see if there is anything beyond. I am drawn in, passing through the flames, they do not touch me, there is no sharp bite of them on my skin.

The light is bright, a constant push on my eyes and I see nothing for the first moments. The noise of the burning tree has disappeared, there is instead the empty rush of space, of air standing still in heat. As my eyes adjust I see short clusters of grass, dry sharp stalks climbing in ragged clumps up the side of a bank of loosening earth, giving way to sand towards its crest. The heat is cloying, pushing at me with a brutish constant force, the air thin with it, I cannot see far, there are dunes to my left and right, behind, a dry bank of crumbling stone and earth that makes a fading edge between trees and sand.

Climbing carefully to the top of the nearest dune, the sand begins to fold itself around my feet, running into my shoes. I feel the grit of it between my toes, I am sweating by the time I reach the top and there is no lightening of the air, no breeze to cool me. Lines and waves of dunes spread into the distance. Instinctively I look for a darker line nearer the horizon, something that speaks of the sea but there is nothing except the hazy air wavering above all this sand and grass.

I do not know what to do and the absence of knowing fills me with a slow, insistent panic building in my chest like the heat that wraps itself around me. There is no path, no place, no landmark to give me a direction. Just these dunes and the line of trees behind me stretching into each distance to my left and right.

It is the heat and the light that pushes me down the slope, back into the still bowl of air that gathers where the base of surrounding hills join, where the sand has the more reassuring feel of earth. Somewhere there is a sun though the sky is a flat, white sheet of light, pouring heat across my shoulders, around my neck.

Down here the air does not move, the silence has a muffled quality to it and in its blankness I begin to pick out something, a dry click or snapping, dull around the edges, uneven and with no rhythm. It is there just on the edge but it gives me something to focus on. It is the sound of wood on wood, stone on stone. Bone on bone. The sudden thought of it clutches at me and I move, walking towards the rise of the next dune, using the movement to shake the thought loose.

I do not know if I am moving towards the sound, it sits in the air around me but its dry, insistent presence remains in the hollows and I skirt the crests of each dune to keep the sound around me, not wanting it to be lost in the wider air above. I keep moving out into the dunes. I do not know how time is passing and it feels as if I have been walking for a long time though the light has not changed, there is no suggestion of a day turning around me. My shirt is wet with sweat and I take it off, tucking it into my waistband. The heat crawls hungrily across my stomach, the curving of my lower back.

That noise continues, it is all around me but I detect a firming of it, a drawing near. There is less distance between us now. I have a choice. I can climb the next dune or I can walk around its base. Whatever is making the noise is the other side. I choose the lower path, wanting the land to be around me. In the next hollow the sand has formed a solid, wide and rough clearing, in the centre, a fire, the flames running quickly up the twisted driftwood piled into a rough pyramid. There is little sound, a quiet soft crack of dry wood as it burns, it is the sound of a fire that has burned long, settled into itself. The dry clicking I have been following is not coming from the fire, it has a higher tone. A figure sits the other side of the flames. Although I had in some sense expected it, I stop, feeling my heart in my ribs. The flames and the heat blur the shape, smear the air between us. I can see broad, bare shoulders, dark hair. His arms flickering with sharp, small movement. I cannot see his face, he is concentrating on something in front of him, hidden to me.

I stand, watching him. The gull's cry is a sudden wrenching from the moment. The man looks up, following the curving arc of the distant bird as it crosses above us. The clicking noise stops and the man is still concentrating on the air above. Then, slowly, he turns his face towards me and I see him through the flames, broad, plain, the lips full and dark, his eyes are in shadow. He stands slowly and I see the thickness of him, the heavy arms and chest, the strong legs. His skin is unadorned, plain, naked. He holds in each hand a rough stone, their edges sharp, rough. He watches me and I feel myself assessed, scrutinised.

He says something, steady words though not ones I know, a soft language, the sounds rounding in the throat and mouth but there are edges, a darkness to them, constrained force, the beating of an ocean on a soft beach. I stand watching him, saying nothing. He repeats the words. The gull cries again, further off now, out in the broader sky where sea and land have merged. I can just hear, out in the edges, the empty rush of the sea, beyond all this hot and shifting sand.

The man moves, coming round the fire towards me, repeating the words. I recognise the cadence of them. I do not move. I sense my shoulders turn to meet him as he steps close. He is my height and his eyes emerge from the shadow, steady and pale. He is still holding the flints, loosely at his sides. As he comes within touching distance I can smell him, a smell of the wide sea, the flat metallic air of the coast, the dark earth that lies beyond it all. He is waiting for my answer but all I do is look at him, unable to hold my eyes to his for long. I am aware of his nakedness though it is me who feels awkward and wrong, my shorts and shoes out of place, my chest pale.

He turns away from me, with a soft grunt that is part exasperation, part judgement and squats facing the fire. He gestures to me to do the same and I crouch next to him. He strikes the two rocks together, steadily, with a practiced force. Small fragments of slate fly away, lost into the sand beneath us. He says something, looking at the fire, then at me, different words this time, a steady statement or observation.

The fire burns and he places a piece of wood on it from a nearby pile. He reaches easily and confidently over to select a piece. The air has thickened with evening now, its coolness shifting the light into darker purples. Off towards the sea the first smears of orange bleed into the sky, as if the fire itself has caught at the horizon's edges. The air loses some of the ferocity of its earlier heat though it still sits deep within my skin. The man has not moved, sitting on his haunches next to me. Occasionally he looks at me and I cannot shake a sense that he is waiting and it is he who is watching to see what this other strange person will do.

There are more gulls now, their cries filling the settling light. The bitter smell of the sea begins to fill this hollow, creeping around the woodsmoke, the hot sand. As light fades, the firelight picks the two of us out in sharper detail. I dare not stare too long at him and, in truth, there is little more to see beyond his skin, the dark hair, the steady, patient striking of the flints.

Then, as the sky deepens into its purpling evening, the man stops striking the stones and looks around and up. He stands and examines the edges of the sand dunes, running his gaze along their tops. He places the flints carefully by the wood pile and walks towards the tallest dune. He extends an arm back towards me, signalling me to follow, saying a single word. I follow and as we reach the base of the dune he suddenly stops, turning to look at me. He is looking at my shorts and he points to them, then taps his chest and he brushes his hands across his thigh. I push the trainers off my feet, undo my shorts to let them drop. He is climbing steadily to the top of the dune and when I am also naked, I follow.

The rim of the world is marbled with the dark red of the last sunlight and above us are the purples, blues and blacks of the first night. There are stars, the brightest ones appearing at our back, bending towards us in the curve of the heavens. Ahead the dunes are bright waves, their undulating slowness cresting before a dimmer, flatter stretch of curving sand and the restlessness of the sea. There is a breeze, it teases at my skin, though the heat of the day still pushes up at me from the sand. We stand and he looks out, not to sea, but to the south where a darker line between land and sky marks out a rising outcropping of land, the cliffs and rocks softening into the night. He watches this carefully. The land and the sea are full of movement, all around us the earth, the air, the tide, they all move their slow and inevitable pattern.

He makes a small sound and places a hand on my bare shoulder, the heat of him briefly pulling me back into this moment. He points to the distant outcrop and there, in the dark, a light flickers, a small twist of orange. It grows steadily and I realise it is a flame, climbing and twisting into the night until a steady bonfire is blazing at the cliff's edge. Its sharp light is hard, quick and sudden against all this dark space.

He turns to the north, swinging his outstretched arm in an arc until it stops at another, flatter promontory of the land, its brow a knuckling of rock. There another flame begins to flicker, dancing into a fury of light and quick, sharp snapping, sparks set loose into the sky. His hand is still on my shoulder and it tightens. He says something, low, forceful. I do not know whether it is a question or a naming. I watch the two beacons. He gives my shoulder a gentle shake and says the words again. This time, sensing the question in it, I look at him. His face is hardly visible in the dark but I know he is watching me. I look at the beacon in the south and nod, not knowing what to do, only that an acknowledgement is needed. He repeats his words, shaking my shoulder again. There is an urgency now to his voice, he wants a response. I look at the northern fire, its light has lit the nearest rocks, their huge, flat curves streaked with shadow.

Suddenly he has stepped in front of me, close, both hands on my shoulder. I feel the heat of him all along my body. He smells like the border of the land, the slick seaweed buried in the fissures of rocks wetted at each tide, the dry earth and dust upon the brittling grasses. His breath is warm across my lips, he asks again, pushing me back and down, the force of it making me step backwards. The slope of the dune catches me off guard and I stagger. I am on one knee now and he follows me down, pushing me into the hollow, the light from the fire lights his face and I do not understand what I see there, the eyes, the forehead wrinkled down in concern but the lips drawn back from the teeth, enough to show their whiteness in the glow. He says the words again, there is an insistence, an urgency and force in them but not anger. He pushes me again and I collapse backwards into the sand. I feel the weight of him settle on my waist, my stomach, his legs holding my ribs and he has leaned his weight forward onto each shoulder. I become aware of our nakedness, the heat of him, of me. I feel the urge of my body responding and I suddenly wonder what this will be. He shakes me, those words again, this time trailing into a thin sound of desperation and he rolls off me, standing, climbing up and out of the dunes into the sky that has quietly filled with stars.

The gull has returned, somewhere out amongst the sands, its long cry soaking into the sands, washing over me lying here. It calls again, harder edged this time, a longer cry that draws out into a howl. My skin tightens, it is my body that recognises that call first. My heart is already pushing urgently at my skin and I stand. My shorts are nearby and I pull them on. There is no sign of the man, no silhouette against the sky to mark him.

Again that cry, sharper in my ears. I cannot mark where it is coming from, the dunes feel full of it and I begin to let my instinct turn me towards the land, to run into the dark of the dunes, seeking solid rock and earth beyond. Just as I am about to leave the light of the fire, the cry comes again but another answers, a solid voice, a single word drawn out. Up there on the dune's crest I see the man, the shape of him, arms outstretched towards me, pushing at something behind me. Again the howl and again the man's response, a low, long note. The figure lowers one arm and, with the other, points towards the south, towards the beacon burning brightly against the darkening skies. I run, into the dunes, towards the land's climbing, towards the fire.

The slope makes a determined surge upwards, towards the cliff top. I can hear the land falling away from me, the crashing of waves reaches me now, breaking over my gasping breath. I am sweating despite the persistent wind that sweeps over the cliffs and pushes at me. The bonfire is above me, a great blaze of restless light. As I climb closer the night is pushed away by it until everything is the sharpness of its red and orange. The noise of the burning fills the sky, rushes round the cropping rocks. I stop, bracing my hands on my knees to draw breath and its roaring fills my head, I hear nothing else, the howls and the responding cries are below me, in the dunes, the fire has burned them away.

I walk past the flames and stand with the heat of it pushing at my back, at the cliff's edge. The night has soaked the sea, the cliffs and there is only shadow and empty space. It would be so easy to take another step, the darkness below would seem to support me. I sense this is what could happen but I have nothing after that, just a dark space.

My breathing settles and I feel the light tracing of sweat towards the waistband of my shorts. I do nothing. I am expecting the shrill bursting of the howl behind me but the night remains full of the crack and rumble of the flames. One of the longer pieces of wood settles deeper into the heart of the fire, there is a rattle of sparks briefly into the sky.

I wait. I close my eyes.

When I open them, the soft lights of the the distant seaside town mark the curve of the coast. Thin, delicate strains of light cross the flat-lands below me, edging the larger roads, tangling around the villages and farms. The night is cool, the air is light, full of space and breeze. I take in a deep breath of it. The bark of the oak is pressing at my spine, the roughness of it a small violence against my skin.

There is an ache in my chest. A breath rises suddenly, I give a cough, a small noise of loss, something snatched away. In the back of my throat I taste smoke and sand and the oiliness of the edge of land and sea.

Chapter 11
Library

The library is fading, a place increasingly forgotten. There are attempts, here and there to bring it back. There is a small area with a few toys scattered across a lively, multi-coloured mat. Amongst the toys are books, their battered covers and rough corners made dimmer and older by the lively brightness around them. A poster has been placed in one of the glass panelled doors, it shows teenagers lying on the grass, each with a book propped against a hand or the leg of a neighbour; one of them wears glasses. Despite these dabs of colour, underneath it all there is still a sense of a library, a quiet gathering of books that have pushed against each other for years.

I walk down the row marked sci-fi and fantasy, the sign is a curling piece of card pushed into a dull, copper holder fixed to the edge of the tall shelf. Although I am looking at the books as I walk slowly up the row, I am playing the role of library user and the titles do not register. I walk with what I intend to be a thoughtful arch of my neck, tilting to read titles of brown, black or faded spines, their edges picked away by years of sliding into shelves, bags, hands.

I am familiar with libraries. On our frequent trips to town my mother would drop me into the muted light of one while she went off to the shops. It was the first place I was left on my own, my first sense of being a person complete in the eyes of anyone who encountered me, not as part of someone else's life. I am aware, as I pretend to stop to examine a book more closely, that I am expected to hold a nostalgia for this place, or each place like it, am supposed to have it weaved tightly into me. I feel none of that.

This library is not as large as the one in the city where we used to live, further north. I recall that one holding its dim light steady throughout the year, full of rows and stacks set out around a central desk, the ceiling lost in the shadows. This library is more confined, less wrapped in its history, placed here in a single room perhaps as a more recent move. The shelves are varnished pine, the floors a bland linoleum. There is still that smell of years, caught in every page but the light is younger.

Sash is not around today. She is seeing Amber. I do not know where they go though I expect it will be local. Sash is spending more time with Amber though she and I still see each other regularly, we arrange ourselves, our plans around that. It would be tempting to say it has changed things between us but it has not.

There is a corner where the back shelves do not quite meet. It is the furthest part from the reception desk, away from the play area and the reading table and the three lumbering PCs. The gap between the shelves is just enough to show the plain walls as they meet, the thin functional pine skirting board. The lino has curled at the very edge. I find myself staring at this gap, uneasy in its existence, the interruption of the line of shelves, the suggestion of the building beyond. A child's quick squeal from near the main doors breaks through and I instinctively turn to the nearest shelf, begin examining the books. They are a worn assortment of local histories, some no more than pamphlets, their spines a folding of the pages and a staple, each move or cataloguing picking away at them. Tucked between a spiral-bound history of local mills and a dark, older book without its dust-jacket there is a slim pamphlet, the jade of its cover marking it out. It is not sitting squarely, as if it has been half-lifted from its place and then abandoned, it tilts towards me and I find myself going to straighten it but the books are tightly packed and I have to push its neighbour away to loosen it enough to move.

'Tales of the Silver Valleys', its title is faintly ornate script, the 'T' curling at its edges, the curve of the 'S' thinning into a flourish. I take it out and lay it flat on my palm. There is a rough ink sketch of a landscape on its cover and I recognise the folding valleys that surround the town, though the town itself is absent. Instead there is a tent, a campfire and a horse in the gentle settling land where the market square is today. The author is a C J Johns. The library's reference sticker has curled away at its edges though it still wraps itself around the thin spine. I open it. The text is solid, functional and the pages have no sense of use, the wholeness of them stands out in the quiet light of the library. There is a sub-title halfway down the page 'The Old Man of Bythall Valley' and below another ink drawing of a hooded figure sitting on a rock, the face left in the shadows. Around him, the flat waters of a pool, the edge of something larger, though the illustrator has no space to do anything other than suggest its presence. The text below, neat unhurried 'Extending in a westerly line from the heart of these valleys, Bythall Valley would have once been wooded, the lakes that are there today not yet formed, certainly the manor house as yet not even an idea. It is in this Valley that the Old Man of Bythall was said to have lived, though exactly where is never revealed.'

The edge of the page is trembling and it distracts me. The hushed sounds of the library wash back in and I look down the aisle towards the door. Everything is normal.

The librarian on the desk does not look at me until he returns the book after he has scanned it, his smile has been used many times before. There is a mother and child now, sprawling on the colourful mat and I smile dutifully at them as I push the door open. Outside the day is a dreary grey, the cloud even and sullen, the heat caught in the narrowing space between, the air still and full of the suggestion of rain. I automatically reach for my phone, the text to Sash half written before the screen comes to life but I stop, remembering where she is, who she is with. The cafe is not very busy and I pick one of the tables down the side. The coffee is hot and while I let it cool I pull the book out of my bag. Its cover looks more worn, more like a hastily printed leaflet here in the light, here by itself against the wood of the table and the neat, white cups and plates.

I read about the Old Man. It is brief story, a local tale with the familiar notes of cautionary wisdom and threat. It seemed to thrive in the early part of the seventeenth century, as the lands, the woods of this particular valley were hardening towards sheep farming, as walls become about boundaries and ownership, as the rivers became sources of power for the mills. The Old Man would be discovered by lost travellers sheltering from storms, from the dark night, in a local cave. There would be a warning given, dire consequences that, if dismissed, would see the traveller lost forever, wandering eternally. The story was vague, the cave's location left unexplained, the Old Man just a presence, emerging from the rock and earth.

I am not surprised when I read the author's biography, neat and succinct on the back page, a young academic, with good pedigree, ambitious to revive and refresh how history is taught and experienced. There is no photograph but I know its our Mr Johns. The book was printed ten years ago.

I sit for a while looking across the cafe, drinking my coffee. The market square is not busy and the people and cars that cross it do so with the bright pace of errands, of purpose. Then there is rain, flecking and spitting at the windows, steadying into an even, soft beating. The smell of the pavement, the wet cobbles, pulses quickly through the door, the heat that lay in the earth now rising. I sit and watch and do nothing.

Chapter 12
The Catcher

Another hot night. This heat arrived a few days ago, oozing into the valleys, sticky and slow, and has settled into the stone and brick of the house, making the rooms smell of carpet and dust and people. An even, unmoving layer of cloud has wrapped itself around each horizon, pushing the heavy air into every corner, every shady place until, if I think too hard about it, the breath becomes firm in my throat.

I am in my room, lying on the bed staring at the low ceiling. The window is open but the sound of the stream seems muffled, clogged by the heat. The house is quiet now but it is thick with a sense of brooding, of the catching web of an argument left unresolved, of words still to be said. If I choose I can hear the muted sound of the TV downstairs, the regular, thin burst of flat laughter.

I close my eyes. When it came, my father's anger was a short thud of rage. He flung the letter across the table at me.

"If you don't sign the fucking form, you can forget about your college fees" he said, each word a restrained blow. He got up sharply and quickly from his chair, toppling it back against the kitchen unit and headed for the door. As he passed the fridge, he raked his hand down the front, ripping the photos and magnets onto the floor. The violence of it broke across us all. My brother flinched, dropping his fork onto his plate. I sat looking at the table in front of me. The final burst of the kitchen door slammed and cracked in my head. The heat and the cloying air of the evening rushed in and smothered it all back to silence. I took another mouthful of my food, chewing carefully though not tasting it.

"Come on" said my mother "Sign it now and your father will settle down." It was not meant to comfort me but to instruct me. She retrieved the form from where it had settled on the floor, placing it in front of me with the pen she kept on the dairy in the corner.

I put down my knife and fork. My brother was watching me, his eyes wide.

"Sign the bloody form, Dan, and stop being so … oh … so bloody stubborn." my mother said. She got up and removed my plate, still half full and it crashed onto the drainer behind me. The noise pushed me out of my stillness and I left the kitchen then, quickly. I know I said 'fuck off' but now, lying here in the gathering darkness, I cannot remember if I said it to them or to myself.

My head is full of noise, the fierceness of my father's voice, the rip of paper, the crash of doors, the clatter of plates, all jarring in my head, obscuring anything else, pushing away any ability to think beyond this moment until they seem to merge, all into one thin, rising cry that lifts from the dark and fills the room, until I must close my eyes to it, turning to face the wall, covering my head with my arms. I give one cough, catching the sob that started to build beneath my ribs, holding it there, though tears have formed and the hotness of them tracks down my nose.

The evening has turned itself towards the night, the last light brushing at the window frame. The noises from the house are of people going through their bedtime routine. My brother, his clumsy closing of the bathroom door. Later the quieter sounds of my father, his steps soft, assured in their routine, his bedroom door just a brief brushing of the wood on thick carpet. I lie there through it all. Later still the clatter of my mother as she rattles toothbrushes and closes the bathroom cabinet too hard, too briskly. I hear her stop in the hallway and I hold my breath but she moves on, closing the door to her own room with the brief, loud rattle of the loose door knob. The house goes quiet, though I am aware it is full of people, each breathing into their sleep, each settling in their own way.

My room is lit with a dim blue light, my phone marking a message. It is from Sash.

"Are you up?"

I am not sure what to say so I let the phone rest alongside my leg, my hand loosely covering it. The curtains lift with the first suggestion of a breeze. This time I feel the buzz of the next message against my thigh.

"I think I got dumped"

And there's an emoji, a shocked face. I lay there and let the dying day finally turn away, watching my mind replay and repeat everything that has happened, reaching out to drag into its endless cycling, the pool, the dancers in the square, the dark brutal weight of the man in the dunes, my father's impassive face, the silhouette of Mr Hardy, Sash's toes in a stream. There, amongst it all, is the icy hill, the Chaser reaching into the cold sky.

I lie there and watch it all twist and turn past me and there is a sort of weight pressing my shoulders to the bed, an insistent heaviness blooming across my stomach and across the tops of my legs. Somewhere out in the night a quick, sharp screech of an owl jars me from the inner twisting of my thoughts.

I pick up my phone, I need to answer, it is expected, needed.

"Can we talk?" And I press send quickly, as if flinging it away before I can alter it. Within seconds the phone hums with

Sash's call but the thought of breaking the silence of the house fills me quickly with panic and I push decline.

"I mean can we meet?"

"What. Like now?"

"Yes. Can you? At our bench maybe?"

There's a slightly longer pause, then "Sure. Give me 30mins"

Leaving the house at night is not easy and I am aware, with every step, of my mother's ability to detect anything her sons do, as if she anticipates every possible transgression, but as I pass her room I can hear the half-snores somewhere in the dark. The front door is a puzzle of potential noises and I take each turn and twist so slowly, so carefully, each unavoidable noise catching in my throat.

The night is warm, though a cooler air runs up the valley. I push my bike down the lane until I am on the larger road that runs into town and only then do I switch on my lights and swing myself into the saddle. The road runs downhill and I let the bike coast, the noise of its drumming steady on the tarmac, the hard push of the saddle bringing me into this moment only.

Sash is sitting on the bench, the light from the nearest street lamp falls weakly around her, the folding rise of the bushes behind her soak up any light so the bench, Sash, her bike stand out against the dark of them. She is watching me, I can see the paleness of her teeth as she smiles and I push my bike up over the paving edge towards her.

"Well, this is all very exciting" she says. I give a gentle snort of laughter. It feels very exposed here, amongst the empty spaces of the town. The buildings around us are dark, shops and workshops. Tucked away, folded into them will be homes, people sleeping or perhaps up late. The town holds itself still in the dark, passing the hours huddled under the sky, waiting for the first return of light to creep down the hills.

We decide to go up on to the common, above the town. Our bikes seem too loud, too quick in the slow hours but we pass through the final houses at the edge and climb the winding lane of the hill. It is too steep and we push the bikes up through the tree line, our breath heavy with the climb.

The common is a wash of greys and blacks. Clouds curl raggedly above, their thickening edges lined with the moon's light, somewhere above it all. To the east a car, its headlights sharply bright, heading away from us. The sense of space lifts away from me, my breathing settles. Sash is standing, looking up at the moving clouds. We walk, not speaking, pushing the bikes, heading towards the centre, away from the darkening edges of the surrounding valleys.

"I'm sorry you got dumped" I say. Sash nods.

Near the middle of the common there is a dip in the land, the short, stubby grass tilting over its edge. It is a shallow, round hollowing out, the shape of it a ragged circle, too clear to be natural. We lay the bikes down and sit. There has been a small fire here, the dark smudge of its ashes marking the centre. The hollow is not deep enough to hide us from the land, we can see the common running away from us, all around us. Over to the north, there is a gathering of sheep, their shapes picked out against the darker grassland by the saturating moonlight.

"I don't know what we're supposed to do now" says Sash. She has picked up a thin stick from the ashes of the fire, its end charred and fading into ash and she is poking at the earth. "I mean, what? We're supposed to have a moment? I'm supposed to collapse in grief? You rush in to comfort me?" She prods at the large ember left by the last log thrown on the fire. "I don't think so. It wasn't that good."

I do not know if her anger is real, whether Sash is annoyed with her story, or that it has led us to this flat hilltop where there is nothing she wants. I do not respond, I sit and look out over the common, watching the sheep, each moving independently, a few paces at a time. I can just hear the rip of their teeth in the grass. In this moment I am suddenly aware of the clouded sky, the dull, uneven land around us and this shallow hollow, us sitting in the dark. As if through earth and rock, as if straining from the lowering clouds above me, I feel pressure in my stomach, my chest, rising until my tongue feels thick, my mouth full of the glut of it.

"Sash … I want …"

From the corner of my eye I see Sash turn to me, the dusk has taken away the detail of her eyes, her mouth and I sense rather than see the neatness of her face, feel her attention fully turned towards me, waiting. She remains so still and it as if all sound has seeped away into the earth around us.

"I want to …" I try to continue but it is too large for my throat, for my tongue to shape, as if it has been waiting there like unshaped clay and I can feel myself drawn towards it, aching to push my fingers into its yielding firmness. It is strange and familiar and old and new, all at once and I know in that moment it is entirely mine.

The howl is almost expected, as if we both knew it would be with us. It fills the air with a sudden, breaking and ragged noise. The sheep scatter, disappearing into the darker edges. Sash is looking at me, her stick poised mid air between us. Her eyes are wide. I begin to stand up, looking at the bikes. Sash grabs my arm, pulling at me to sit down, shaking her head. She drops the stick and holds up her hand, signalling to me to wait. The silence that swells in to the air after the cry feels thick, full of waiting. The land, the air around us is like a waiting breath.

The next scream seems to last longer. It fills my head, pushing at the back of my throat. It rises and then falls away, as if anger is turning to desperation, a trailing note of pain, until it stops, the night filling with its absence again. Although my heart is beating hard, Sash's hand seems to anchor us both and we sit, each now looking out across the common into the unmoving night.

"What do we do?" I ask, whispering it. We both jump as another cry fills the air around us, pressing us down into the hollow.

"Wait" Sash says "See where its coming from. Then run. The other way."

I sense myself respond to the idea of running, a strong pulse in my legs, readying themselves and I nod in the dark. But there is something else, a flat note of despair ringing steadily through my panic. More running, the Chaser will follow, more flight and scrambling in the dark.

The Chaser's next howl has edges, clear and cold, marked out and full of pain and anger and … that note, this one that has risen inside my chest, my throat, it resonates, combines and I sense some dreadful harmony between us.

"There" Sash says and points to the north, into the darkening grey and there is something pushing towards us, the darkness folding, lumbering as if up from the earth. Sash has taken her hand from my arm and the cool absence of it breaks us apart enough for my thoughts to scramble back from behind the urge to run. That note of despair rings through it all and I hear it flung back to me in the Chaser's next cry, higher, clearer now, coming from that heaving knot of darkness getting closer and I suddenly see us both, there in a hole in the ground, as if from above. I see the land spreading and curving around us and there is no light, no marking of the time, nothing except the incoming tide of an eternal night.

I sense Sash preparing to run, the small movements, the shift in her weight and the slight rising of her body as she braces her feet.

"Sash, wait" I say and it is me who reaches to her, my hand on the top of her arm "Wait. Don't."

I cannot see her face but I sense the confusion in the turn of her head towards me.

"What the …?" she says, her voice no longer a whisper.

The Chaser's next scream is long, loud, it rushes through us and though it seems full of anger and triumph, that single note of something else is still there and I grasp it, using it to pull me up, standing and moving on legs that would rather run towards the edge of the hollow, away from where the dark has folded itself into a tall gaunt shape, its long arms reaching out towards me and when its next scream pushes itself out from deep within it, I feel myself echoing it, letting it push something up from my belly, up my spine and drawing from every rib, out into the night to wrap itself into the Chaser's cry. It is long and ragged and I feel the whole earth and the common, the trees and the valleys full of it and I open my chest, my mouth, releasing them until I can feel the resonance of it in every bone, into the muscle and skin. There is only this, here in the world, only this.

Chapter 13
An Ending

I try not to recall that night too often these days. It seems as a story now, told to frighten kids, and in its telling and re-telling, it risks being flattened, worn down into something caught between pages quickly forgotten amongst many other stories. I have stopped telling it now and no-one seems to notice.

Usually I end the story with a terrible confrontation, Sash and I standing our ground, there on that dark common, the huge shape of the Chaser pulling itself from the dark, raising its jointed arms above us as it grasps and clambers into the hollow. Usually I tell how Sash begins to scream, her own howl joining mine until it seems as if all the years ahead of us have come into this moment and flood the air around us, the harsh cry of the Chaser a jarring tangle of noise amongst it all. Usually the story ends with it fading into darkness, like smoke that hovers just before a breeze pushes through it, smudging it into the air. I leave us both there, sitting close together, not speaking. Sash lights a fire, or sometimes it is me, and we sit looking at its small brightness flickering against the night. The first light of day curls itself around the eastern edge of the common and the darkness turns first to greys and blues until eventually it seems the light from our fire has spread itself out under the thin clouds above, brushing against their folding edges and then … then the sun.

It is not a bad ending, as endings go, although I am often asked about the Chaser, whether it has truly gone, whether it has now been pushed from the world. I say something vague, hoping to appear enigmatic, fulfilling my role as story teller. I never point out to them that their question implies a final victory, that Sash and I in some way defeated it. I never tell them that they have focused on the wrong ending, that in their fascination with the monster, they have missed the story. In the re-telling of it, I have almost come to believe this ending myself. Sometimes I see the small thrill in someone's face as they decide that the Chaser may still be out there in the valleys, the woods, along the hilltops, that it will always reappear in the rituals amongst the drums and that endlessly looping melody.

Occasionally, perhaps as I sit in the moment between leaving the venue, the store, the hall and the starting of my car, in that small moment I might remember how it did not feel like an ending at all. The world crept back into that next day, the air restless with coming warmth, a van climbing out of the next valley to clatter along the narrow road, the sheep loosely clustered nearby. The world went on in its grinding way. Sash and I did not speak, we pushed our bikes towards the edge of the common, pausing to look over the town below. There was a sense of falling away, as if everything that had been around us was now revealed as thinner, less likely to carry us and that we dare lean on what we knew in case it became as smoke.

I miss Sash. Our lives simply wound away from each other over the years that followed. We exchange a text perhaps once a year, it usually suggests getting back together over coffee. That never happens. I wonder how she is, whether she still pushes off her shoes to dip her feet in streams. She has a daughter now, only a few years old, and a wife, though I've never met either of them. I once saw her on social media, the three of them standing next to a large, plastic pink dinosaur, Sash looking down at her small daughter in her arms, another woman, taller, her arms loosely around Sash's shoulders, leaning in to kiss Sash on the cheek, long, curling hair hiding most of her face.

We gather stories around our selves, they place us each at the centre. Too often we create our stories to reflect the light of those around us and, in doing so, impose them on the world until eventually they sit among all the other stories, like delicate collections placed on shelves already tight with other anthologies, so packed in they become indistinguishable, difficult to tease out. If we're not careful, we miss the stories that already exist, are already there, seeped into the land, hanging in the air. These are the wilder ones, the uncertain ones, their meanings so spread about us they are like the deep, gripping roots of trees that creep around the stone, through the earth, not seen, not understood. If we only listen to our own stories, the earth becomes as a shadow.

Those moments of remembering are getting less frequent now, perhaps as newer stories crowd in. Sometimes I wonder if I should write it down. In the many silent hours when the library is not busy, when I am surrounded by the hanging air of books, I feel an urge creep into my chest to write the true story, the one without the ending. Usually I just sit and wait and eventually it goes away or the library door opens and there is a brief, soft tumble of noise from the world outside and I close my notebook, leaving perhaps my hand gently on its cover as I smile at the person approaching the desk.

More from Innes Richens:

An Allowance of Small Noises

Sometimes we observe the world and notice the host of small detail that surrounds us. Sometimes, if we allow it, we let the detail in and it can become a story, a moment in some other life or perhaps a memory we wished we held ourselves.

This collection of encounters with people and places from real and imagined worlds touches on the mundane, the imagined, the observed and the arcane. Inspired by postcard stories and flash fiction, these pieces aim to give brief moments of reading. Touching on aspects of our known and unknown world, they are a collection of stories brought together through the collaboration of Valerie Bird, author of 'Incident on the Line' and 'A Retrospective', and Innes Richens, a new writer making his debut here. Each author has extended a real experience to imagine what may have happened, in the hope that the reader is never sure where the truth forms part of the overall fabric of the moment.

Join Innes's email list here:
www.innesrichens.co.uk

Lightning Source UK Ltd.
Milton Keynes UK
UKHW021035300122
397927UK00010B/400